A Brief History of the Baptists and Their Distinctive Principles and Practices

William Cecil Duncan

Contents

A BRIEF HISTORY OF THE BAPTISTS AND THEIR

DISTINCTIVE PRINCIPLES AND PRACTICES

BY

William Cecil Duncan

PREFACE.

THE History of the Early Baptist Church has never yet been written. No book that treats comprehensively of Primitive Christianity, has viewed it, so far as I know, from a Baptist point of contemplation. Such an attempt is made, for the first time, in the present Volume.

In preparing this History, I have had the most scrupulous regard to accuracy; looking at every point in the single light shed upon it by the Scriptures and by History. I am not conscious of having, in any instance, allowed what might be considered my Baptist predilections to influence, much less to direct, my researches for the Truth. Having taken the Scriptures and History as my guide, I have registered in the following pages, in a brief yet comprehensive manner, the results of my study and reflection on the doctrines and usages of the Early Baptist Church.

I believe that not only all the leading, but all the subordinate, positions taken in this book, are strictly Baptist. Certain it is, that there is no one of its sentiments which is not entirely concordant with the *distinctive* principles and practices of that denomination. On some points of minor importance, there being room for a candid difference of opinion, the Baptists have no fixed and determinate doctrine. On these, I have felt at liberty to discourse with perfect freedom; not attempting to give,—what, in the nature of the case, can not be determined, and what, if it *were* determined, ought not, in any way, to bias the mind of a history-writer,—the present opinion of the majority of Baptists; but stating the conclusions which my own mind has reached after an independent and pains-taking investigation. No topic have I treated hastily; but have bestowed upon each a scrupulously careful examination. It has been my object to make a *true* rather than an immediately *popular* History; being firmly convinced, that, though error may meet with favor for a time, the truth alone can stand the fiery trial of a rigid scrutiny, and live in coming years.

This book professes to be Part First of a "Brief History of the Baptists" in all ages. It is also an independent work; containing a compendious account of the History and of the Distinctive Principles and Practices of the Apostolic and ***Early Baptist Church.*** Another volume, bringing the History down to our own day, will be added in due time, if found advisable.

I have endeavored to make this Treatise a hand book of the History and Usages of the Primitive Baptist Church. If it bring to those who read it the same pleasure and profit it has brought to him who wrote it, I shall be content.—Go forth, then, child of labor, child of prayer; and mayst thou meet with a kind reception from candid and truth loving hearts.

AIM AND OBJECTS OF THE HISTORY.

THE object of the present Treatise is to give a concise history of the Baptists, and their distinctive principles and practices, from the "beginning of the Gospel" down to our own day. Baptists do not, as do most Protestant denominations, date their origin from the Reformation of 1520. By means of that great religious movement, indeed, they were brought forth from comparative obscurity into prominent notice; and, through it, a new and powerful impulse was given to their principles and practices in all those countries which had renounced allegiance to the Pope of Rome. They did not, however, originate with the Reformation; for long before Luther lived, nay long before the Roman Catholic Church herself was known, Baptists and Baptist churches existed and flourished in Europe, in Asia, and in Africa.

The word "Baptist" signifies a ***baptizer.*** The Baptists therefore are, emphatically, they who baptize. They are so called from their practice of immersion as alone Baptism, and from the distinctive articles of their religions belief. The doctrine by which they are fundamentally distinguished from all other professing Christians is, and has always been, the following: ***Christian Baptism is the immersion in water of a believer in Christ, by a properly authorized administrator, in the name of the Father, Son, and Holy Spirit***(Matt. 28: 19), ***or in the name of Jesus*** (Acts 8: 16; 19: 5). From this doctrine is directly deducible another, as a corollary from a mathematical demonstration: ***Infant Baptism is unscriptural, and a perversion of the ordinance of Christ.***

These two doctrines have been in all ages the distinguishing principles of some part of the professed Church of God; and that part—called at one time by one name, and at another time by another—so long as it has held fast to these principles, and the practices legitimately based upon them, has been composed of Baptists. Those Christians, then, who have observed and advocated these fundamental doctrines respecting the nature of Baptism, and the persons to whom it is to be administered—admitting, on the one hand, nothing to be baptism but immersion, and, on the other, administering the rite to those only who have made a credible profession of faith in Christ—wherever, and in whatever age they are found, provided that in other things also they take the Scriptures as the guide of their faith and practice, these, by whatever appellation known, are genuine Baptists. It is the history of such, and of their principles and practices, which is concisely presented in this "Brief History of the Baptists."

There are other doctrines of a highly important, but not necessarily fundamental, character, at present held and practised by Baptists everywhere throughout the world; but as they are not, at this day, strictly speaking, ***distinctive*** sentiments of that people, since they are held also by other Christians; and as the evidence on which they rest is not susceptible of so clear and satisfactory a statement, and is not—at least as far as regards that early period of Baptist history which is included between the decease of the Apostle John (100 A. D.) and the death of Origen (254, A. D.)—by any means so conclusive, or so generally admitted by ecclesiastical historians, as the proof adduced in favor of Baptist views respecting the act and subjects of Baptism, it would scarcely be proper to enumerate them as doctrines peculiar to the Baptists, or as principles to which every Baptist, to be such, must of necessity subscribe.

One of the chief of these doctrines has reference to the nature of ecclesiastical organization, that is, to Church Polity; respecting which Baptists hold, and have held from an early period, that the churches of Christ are independent of one another, each having power to choose its own officers and to administer its own affairs, without the intervention of a diocesan bishop, or any other territorial ecclesiastical functionary.—Partly in consequence of this view of theirs respecting ecclesiastical polity, but more particularly as the result of the yet more important doctrine of their belief, that the Church of Christ must be composed of baptized believers alone, Baptists have, in every period of the history of Christianity, been preeminently distinguished, wherever found, for their opposition to any and every kind of alliance between the Church and the State, and for their advocacy of unrestricted freedom in matters of religion. "Liberty of conscience" has been their watch-cry in every age. For this they have testified, and suffered, and died. They were the first of modern times to assert the doctrine in its plenitude; and they did so when all other Christians, Protestants as well as Catholics, were casting fetters around the religious spirit, and binding it to a rigid conformity with legally established doctrines and ceremonies.

Such as have been enumerated are the principles, for which Baptists are distinguished. The history of these principles is briefly unfolded in the following chapters, and, as far as may be, the history also of the most distinguished characters by whom they have, at different periods, been advocated and the area of their influence extended. The doctrine that immersion alone is baptism and that believers alone are entitled to receive the rite, and the practices necessarily arising from this religious conviction, are the essential and distinctive elements of Baptist usage and belief. They will, therefore, constitute the thread by means of which we shall guide our progress through the long labyrinth of ecclesiastical and religious history, and the central point around which our representations shall revolve. Light will be thrown, in the course of the investigation, upon all the more important principles and practices of those who have professed and acted upon Baptist belief; but all the rays of that light will be made to converge on a common focus—a representation of the ***distinctive and fundamental*** doctrines and usages of Baptists in every period of the history of Christianity.

Whoever, in any age of Christianity, has held to the fundamental doctrines and usages which have been mentioned, he is rightly called a Baptist. And he is such, whatever, in other respects, may have been his doctrinal belief and practices. Baptism is the initiatory ordinance of the Christian Church; and he who has rightly received it, is a member of the visible—not necessarily, however, of the invisible— body of Christ. He may hold erroneous sentiments respecting a number of doctrinal points and points of ecclesiastical usage; yet, if he be sound on those doctrines upon which is raised the superstructure of the visible Church, he is a Baptist; an imperfect and erring one, it may be, but still a Baptist. Being such, his history is interwoven with that of the great body of the Baptists who have flourished, or suffered, in different periods of the Christian dispensation, and must be considered in a treatise which, like the present, purports to be a general "History of the Baptists and of their Distinctive Principles and Practices."

In our review of this history, we shall begin with the first establishment of the Church of Christ; and from that point shall descend, by successive steps, to the present time. We shall find that for two hundred and fifty years Baptist doctrines and the doctrines of all Christendom respecting the act and the subjects of Baptism, are identical; that then corruption began its work in the Church, and, as regards at least the subjects of the baptismal rite, extended, within a few centuries, to the greater part of the Christian world; leaving only a comparatively small minority to uphold and practise the pure principles of the New Testament; that subsequently, for twelve hundred years, the true Church was persecuted, and its members hunted down in every land, but that neither it nor they were utterly destroyed; that, at length, on the coming of the Reformation, Baptists, though still persecuted, emerged in every Protestant country, from their valleys and hiding-places, and after passing through much tribulation, took a prominent position in the religious world, and entered upon that career of internal and external progress for which they are distinguished among the Christian denominations of modern times. This progress has been most rapid among the nations of Anglo-Saxon blood and Anglo-Saxon institutions; and from these, Baptist principles and Baptist practices seem destined to go forth, in ever-increasing power, until they shall have penetrated and subdued the entire religious and heathen world. A sketch of the history of such principles, if faithfully delineated, can not be otherwise than valuable, and, to a Christian mind, highly interesting and attractive.

PART FIRST.
FROM THE "BEGINNING OF THE GOSPEL" TO THE RISE OF AFFUSION (POURING)
AS BAPTISM, AND OF INFANT BAPTISM, 28 A. D.—250 A. D.

CHAPTER I.
AGE OF CHRIST: FROM THE FOUNDING OF THE CHURCH
TO THE ASCENSION, 28—31, A. D.

The First Baptizer—"John the Baptist"—The "First Beginnings of the Christian Church"—The Call of the Apostles—The Baptism administered by the Disciples in the Jordan, during the Ministry of the Forerunner—Relation of John's to Christian Baptism—Summary of the Arguments in Favor of the Identity of John's Baptism and the Christian Ordinance—John's Baptism and Ministry, be they what they may, do not affect-our View of the Church and its Baptism—The Opinion that the Apostles must themselves have received the Christian Rite—The Apostles, under Christ, the Founders of the Church—Number of Baptisms previous to the Ascension—The "Apostolic Commission"?An Extension of the Commissions given to "the Twelve" before the Crucifixion.

THE first baptizer was John the Baptist. In the year of Rome 752, Tiberius being on the throne of the Cæsars, that holy man came forth from the wilderness of Judea "into all the country about (the) Jordan, preaching the baptism of repentance for the remission of sins." He appeared as the forerunner of the Messiah, "to make ready a people prepared for the Lord"; and to give his testimony in favor of the Messiah, when he should present himself for recognition. At the proper time our Lord did present himself, and received baptism at the hands of John, in-order that, divine though he was, he might "fulfill all righteousness." Immediately after receiving the ordinance, Jesus went forth from the waters of the Jordan, and retired for a time to the scene of his temptation in the wilderness; but soon reappearing, he entered at once and for all upon the labors of his ministry. John, the apostle, and James, his brother, Andrew and Peter, Philip and Nathaniel (Bartholomew), induced by the testimony of the Baptist given specially to John and Andrew, soon joined themselves to Christ; and were publicly called by him into his discipleship.

The first who acknowledged Jesus as the Messiah were Andrew and John; and they were the *first* disciples. They were, as the pithy Bengel well expresses it, "the first beginning of the Christian Church." In receiving them as his disciples, our Lord laid the foundation of his visible Church. This was the commencement of the formation of that community which, under the name of Apostles, constituted the ground-work of the Christian Church, Christ himself being the chief corner-stone of the building. They, in connection with those who were subsequently chosen, were to be leaders, under Jesus the head, in the kingdom of Christ; and were, after the removal of their Master, to carry out his teachings into practice, and to build up the superstructure of the spiritual edifice whose foundation he himself had laid.

The public call of these Apostles was made during our Lord's first visit to Galilee after his consecration and recognition as the Messiah by John the Baptist. Their labors as co-founders of his Church, together with Christ, began very soon after their call to discipleship. Leaving Galilee with them in companionship, Jesus proceeded to Jerusalem; and thence into the country of Judea, into the neighborhood of Ænon?place situated on the banks of the Jordan, near to Salim?where John was then preaching and baptizing. Here he remained with his disciples from the spring until the following autumn—a period, it is probable, of about eight months. While he tarried here with them, they baptized those who professed belief in the Messiahship of their Master; and the number of the recipients of the rite was so great, that it is stated "Jesus made and baptized more disciples than John"

The account of these transactions is given in John 3: 22, 23, as compared with 4:1, 2. Here is the first mention in the New Testament of a baptism which initiates into and is token of discipleship with Jesus personally, as the Christ. As to external form, it was identical with the rite administered by John—an immersion of the body into water; and, like his, it could be performed only upon persons capable of understanding its import. Both were forms of initiating into and badges of discipleship; and each bound its recipient to the performance of certain prescribed duties. In design and significance, however, the rite administered by our Lord's disciples differed from that performed by John. The latter was administered to its recipient upon a profession of repentance and of faith in a Messiah *about to come;* the former, upon a profession of faith in Jesus as *the* Messiah *already come,* and preaching in his own person "the acceptable year of the Lord" The subjects of the Christian rite professed, by the act of reception, a belief in the Messiahship of Jesus *personally;* and bound themselves, as by an oath, to allegiance to him as "a teacher sent from God," and as their rightful lord and sovereign. By the reception of the ordinance, they were initiated into the community of Christian believers. So much was effected by the rite administered near Ænon by the disciples of our Lord; and the baptism performed by them even after the resurrection of Christ, and after their reception of the Holy Spirit, could, in and of itself, effect no more.

In the age of the Reformers was advocated, for the first time, particularly by Calvin, the doctrine that John's baptism is identical with the Christian ordinance. No ecclesiastical writer before them, however, holds to any such sentiment; all who speak on the subject contending, from the earliest period of Christianity, that the two ceremonies are not the same in significance. Among these are Tertullian, Origen, Chrysostom, Gregory Naziahzen, Augustine (the last in almost six hundred places); and, at a later period, Bede, Anselm, etc. After the time of the Reformers, the opinion that the two rites are identical was held by a number of theologians, until the rise of modern biblical criticism; since which that view has, by general consent, been reversed.

Comparatively few biblical critics, now-a-days, Baptist or Pædo-Baptist, contend for the opinion which had its origin in the times of the Reformation. The diversity of the two baptismal ceremonies, in point of significance, is clearly proved by the express testimony of the Forerunner himself (Matt. 3: 11; Luke 3: 16; John 1: 26); by the facts recorded in John 3: 25, if.; by those (we think) in Acts 19: 1-6, and by other considerations.

The doctrine of the precise identity of John's baptism with that administered by the Apostles after the memorable "day of Pentecost" (that is, with undoubted Christian baptism), is held by many among the Baptists. Such seek to establish their position by the arguments long since used by the eminent Pædo-Baptist Calvin, who contends "that the ministry of John was precisely the same as that which was afterwards committed to the Apostles." Their reasoning is not destitute of force. They rely, in particular, on the fact that Mark speaks of the ministry of the Baptist as "the beginning of the gospel of Jesus Christ" (Mark 1: 1). Reference is also made by them to Matt. 11: 12, 13 (cp. Luke 16: 16), where the ministry of John appears to be spoken of as the commencement of the Christian dispensation. These passages, however, do not, when rightly understood, go to prove that John's baptism and the Christian ordinance are identical. The evidence which they afford is, at best, of a negative kind; while that on the other side is positive.

That John's Baptism is identical with Christian Baptism, though held by very many in the Baptist denomination, is not distinctive Baptist doctrine. Some of the best, and some of the most learned of Baptists have, in times past, held a contrary opinion. Among these are the accomplished and eloquent Robert Hall, who thinks that the ceremonies are "two distinct institutes," (*Works,* vol. 2, p. 20, London edition); and the well-known scholar and controversialist, Alexander Carson, who speaks of the rites as being "in two points essentially different" (*On Baptism,* p. 281, American edition, 32). And it is a question whether, at the present time, even in America, not only the most learned, but the greater number, among our Baptist biblical critics, do not believe that the ordinance administered by John was not precisely the same in significance as that performed by the Apostles on and after "the day of Pentecost."

The view which Rev. Dr. Angus, President of Stepney College, London, has given of John's ministry, in his admirable work entitled "Christ our Life" (pp. 90, 91), shows that he considers the Baptism of the Forerunner not identical with the Christian ordinance. Rev. Prof. Ripley, of Newton Theological Seminary, Massachusetts, in his Notes on the Gospels, (p. 44, edition of '39) says that the "Baptism of John, though it was but the commencement of the New Dispensation, the twilight of the new day, yet contained substantially the elements of the ordinance as still further developed and carried out by the Messiah himself." So Rev. I. T. Hinton (*History of Baptism,* p. 64) regards "the Baptism of John as Christian Baptism in a state incompletely developed." If the rite administered by John needed to be "further developed," it could hardly have been "precisely the same" as Christian Baptism. Any concession here, however small, on the part of those who think that the two rites are in all respects identical, will overthrow the whole fabric of their arguments.

The position of the Baptists in the "Baptismal Controversy" with Pædo-baptists, is not at all disturbed by holding to a diversity between John's Baptism and the Christian ordinance. That **Believers' Immersion** alone is Christian Baptism, is abundantly proved from the practice of Christ's disciples before his death, from the wording of the commission given just before his ascension, and from the subsequent invariable usage of the Apostles. If these considerations, added to the arguments founded on the meaning of the word **baptizo** and its cognates, do not prove that believers' immersion alone is Christian Baptism, neither can it be shown that John's Baptism was the immersion of believers alone; for the facts are established, in each case, by precisely the same kind and the same amount of evidence. John performed an act which is called **baptisma** (immersion); and the act performed by the Apostles is designated by the same term. As to form, then, both ordinances were **immersion.** Neither rites, as far as the New Testament record shows, was in any case, administered to others than believers[1].

It is contended by some, that the baptism administered by Christ's disciples was not Christian; and was nearly, if not quite, identical with the ordinance administered by John. This view, however, can not be sustained; for the baptism performed by the disciples initiated directly into the personal fellowship of Christ, and evidently had his sanction. It was in all respects, save perhaps its direct internal significancy, the same as that administered by the Apostles on the day of Pentecost; for both rites were based upon repentance and belief in Christ Jesus, and both initiated into the Christian Church. Even in respect to its direct internal significancy, the rite which was administered by the disciples **may** have been the same as that performed by them afterwards as Apostles; for it is not impossible, nay, it is rather probable, that it was understood by them, and by those to whom they administered it, as symbolizing that baptism of the Spirit, which, according to John's testimony, the Messiah was to perform.

Jesus himself baptized not. His disciples were, with his approval, and probably by his express direction, the administrators of the Christian rite. To them was the foundation on which the Church was to be built, our Lord entrusted the office of rearing its superstructure, and of introducing into the building, by means of a baptismal consecration, the materials of which it was to be composed. They

---

1   A just view of this point is taken in Prof. Well's hook on "Baptism," (p. 62); and in Rev. J. M. Pendleton's "Three Reasons for Becoming a Baptist "(pp. 111, 112).

were constituted the founders of the Church by a special call from its divine head and lawgiver. Being such, and so called, they needed not to receive themselves the ordinance of baptism; and it must always, from want of satisfactory historical evidence, remain doubtful whether they ever did receive Christian baptism, properly so called. According to Clement of Alexandria (†220)[2],. Christ himself baptized them with his own hands, on admitting them into his fellowship. This assertion of Clement's, however, can hardly be true; else would some mention of the fact— which is not impossible in itself considered—have been made by one or more of the Evangelists. The Christian ordinance, it is most probable, was not instituted until after their call as Apostles; and they were the chosen instruments of its first administration. Their title to the Apostleship which they exercised, was based, not on a baptism performed on them by Jesus, but on the special call which they had received from him as the head of the Church. As apostles, they were, under Christ, the instituters of Christian baptism, and the founders of the new spiritual community over which he, whether in his state of humiliation or exaltation, is the divinely constituted sovereign.

Those Baptists (and they are many in America) who believe that John's Baptism and the Christian ordinance were identical, hold, of course, that the Apostles were initiated into the Church, when they received baptism from the Forerunner. Some think moreover, that, without such a baptismal consecration, the Apostles would not have themselves been qualified to administer the Christian ordinance. This latter view, however, is clearly erroneous; for admitting the premises from which it is derived, it would follow that John, being himself unbaptized, could not have duly administered the rite which he performed. But John's Baptism *was,* it is agreed on all hands, rightly and properly administered; and it *was so,* all say, *because God had sent him to baptize.* In the same way, the "commission" given to the Apostles by Christ was *their* authority for baptizing; and, so commissioned, the baptisms performed by them were valid, even if they had themselves never been dipped beneath the waters of the Christian ordinance.

Whatever may have been the relation of the ministry of John the Baptist to

---

2   The sign † within parenthesis, followed by a date, means that the person just mentioned died in that year. It is used throughout this Treatise for the sake of brevity

the Christian dispensation, and whatever may have been the relation of his baptism to the confessedly Christian ordinance, the view which the student of the New Testament will feel bound to take respecting the Church of Christ and its initiatory ordinance, must remain in either case essentially the same. If John's baptism did initiate into the Church, yet its divine authority ended with the Forerunner himself; it being superseded, or as some say, perfected, by the baptism authorized by the "commission." After this, it was no longer John's but Christ's baptism. If, on the other hand, the rite was merely temporary, it was only a baptismal consecration preparatory to that of the Church; and of course, was done away with, when it had accomplished its end,—the baptism of the Church, independent from the first, still continuing, and being destined to continue till the end of time.

Baptists at large, especially in America, consider John's ministry the beginning of the Christian Dispensation (which it certainly *is* in one sense, if not in theirs); and hold, as has been noticed above, that his Baptism was identical with the Christian ordinance. That this opinion may be fairly represented, we give here a summary of the arguments by which it is sustained. They are stated substantially in the form in which they have been put forth by others: 1.) John's ministry is represented in Mark (1: 1,) as "the beginning of the Gospel;" and, 2.) the Kingdom of Heaven is spoken of in Matthew (11: 12, 13,) and in Luke (16: 16,) as having begun in its visible organization with the ministry of the Baptist. These facts show that John's Preaching and Baptism were on the same footing as Preaching and Baptism at a later period in the Christian Dispensation. 3.) John and Jesus baptized at the same time; which they would not have done, had their baptisms not been identical. 4.) The terms of the Baptism of John were the same as those of the Baptism performed on and after the day of Pentecost, viz.: Repentance and Faith. 5.) John's disciples were not, on becoming followers of Jesus, re-baptized. These are the arguments used by those who consider John's Baptism identical with the Christian rite. How far they are valid, is left for those who are interested in this subject to determine to their own satisfaction. The view which they are supposed to support, whether it be correct or not, is held by very many Baptists at the present day.

It is not to be supposed that the number received by baptism into the personal discipleship of our Lord, was at any time very large. His intention was not to form an extensive visible community during his life; but rather to choose here and there, from among the Jewish nation, and bring into direct fellowship with himself, such persons only as would be, on account of their greater religious susceptibility, the more easily imbued with the spirit of Christianity, and become, after his ascension, fit instruments for the propagation of his religion in Judea and throughout the world. After leaving the Jordan, in the neighborhood of Ænon, the disciples may, or may not, have continued to baptize. That they did so often, or that they at any one time administered to a large number this initiatory ordinance, is hardly reconcilable with the unbroken silence on this point of all the four evangelists. Instead of gathering together an organized community, and adding daily to its numbers and strength, as did the Apostles afterwards, our Lord seems, after this period, during the whole course of his ministry, to have preferred to sow the good seed of the Gospel throughout the provinces of Judea and Galilee; leaving them, as fruit-bearing elements, to spring up and ripen into a harvest for the sickles of the Apostles and disciples who were, after his exaltation, to go "everywhere, preaching the word." The number admitted into his direct discipleship was small. Taken altogether, after the sifting process to which they were subjected on the occasion of the seizure, trial, and execution of their Master, his disciples did not, immediately after his ascension, probably number in all Judea and Galilee, many more than five hundred (cp. 1 Cor. 15: 6).

The narrative of our Lord's personal ministry from the time of his stay on the banks of the Jordan until his death and ascension, is familiar to all who have read the Gospels. Not only did he labor himself, but he sent out the Apostles, "the twelve," and subsequently "the seventy" disciples, to proclaim "to the lost sheep of the house of Israel" the advent of the Messiah and the establishment of his heavenly kingdom upon earth.

After his resurrection Christ solemnly announced, on several distinct occasions, to the Apostles, and through them to the whole Church, the duties which they were thenceforth to perform. "All power," said he to "the eleven" on a mountain in Galilee, "is given unto me in heaven and on earth. Go ye, ***therefore,*** and teach [make disciples from among] all nations, baptizing them in [into] the name of the Father, and of the Son, and of the Holy Ghost; teaching them to observe all things whatsoever I have commanded you: and, lo, I am with you always even unto the end of the world" (Matt. 28: 18-20). The last words which he uttered to the

Apostles, just as he was about to ascend into heaven from Bethany, and his last injunction, previous to blessing them, were to the same effect: "Ye shall be witnesses unto me both in Jerusalem and in all Judea, and in Samaria, and unto the uttermost part of the earth" (Acts 1: 8). This is the "Apostolic Commission," and it is in full force at this present day; as binding as ever upon the Church of God.

This Apostolic Commission was not, as regards the proclamation of the Gospel, something entirely new; something which the Apostles had not heard of before the death of their Master. The apostolic office had already some time since commenced; and they had previously been acting under instructions similar in all essential particulars, except as regarded the people among whom they were to labor. The present was, in truth, only a repetition of the commission which the twelve had previously received. It differed from it only in one important respect. The restriction under which they first proclaimed the Gospel,—a restriction imposed for good reasons,—was now removed. Instead of being confined to "the lost sheep of the house of Israel," the good news of salvation was henceforth to be preached "among *all* nations."

In another note-worthy particular, the so-called Apostolic Commission differed from that given to "the twelve" before the death of their Master. The one last enjoined was an enlargement of the other, not only as regards the persons to whom the Gospel was to be proclaimed, but as regards the formal incorporation of those who believed into the Christian Church. Though the Apostles had the right to administer, and had previously administered Baptism, their original Commission did not instruct them to perform that rite upon those who should believe their proclamation respecting the advent of the Messiah. This injunction,—which is made so prominent in the Commission as enlarged,—was, there is good reason to believe, purposely withheld by our Lord; because the time had not come, when numbers of converts should be admitted within the pale of the outward visible Church. The Apostles therefore, were not commissioned to baptize in the prosecution of their first missionary enterprise. Their work was then only preparatory. They were to go through the cities of Judea and Galilee, and *preach;* saying, "The kingdom of heaven is at hand" (Matt. 10: 7), just as Jesus himself had done, when he commenced his ministry (Matt. 4: 17), before "the twelve" had been specially called as Apostles.

Our Lord, in his notable prayer for the Apostles, distinctly recognizes them as having acted already under his authority, as vicegerents of his in announcing the Gospel. "As thou hast sent me into the world, even so," he says, "*have I also sent them* into the world" (John 17: 18). From this it is clear (if the expression is not to be regarded as proleptic or anticipatery), and it also follows from other considerations, that the Commission given after the resurrection was only a repetition, with amplifications, of instructions previously enjoined by Christ, and previously, acted upon by the Apostles. The Church had already been founded, before the death of the Saviour: the Apostles had initiated into it by baptism, at least for a time; they had preached the Gospel; they had performed miracles; and they had been appointed by Christ the rulers and regulators of the visible "Kingdom of Heaven". They needed yet only to be prepared to proclaim the Gospel among the Gentiles, by the reception of the Spirit, which was to lead them "into all truth"; and to be endowed with a knowledge which would enable them to discriminate between ecclesiastical practices essential, and practices indifferent, and to discern, when necessary, true from false professors, in order that, on the one hand, they might always decide for the best interests of Christianity, and, on the other, might incorporate only fit elements into the building of the Lord. The necessary preparation they received, in full measure, on the day of Pentecost.

CHAPTER II.
THE APOSTOLIC AGE: FROM THE ASCENSION
TO THE DEATH OF JOHN, 31—100 A. D.

§1. OUTWARD DEVELOPMENT OF THE CHURCH.

Its full Establishment on the Day of Pentecost—The First Baptisms under the Spirit's Dispensation—Progress from Jerusalem, after the Death of the Proto-martyr Stephen—The First Gentile Converts—Barnabas and Paul—Paul's Missionary Travels—Death of Paul and Peter—The Labors and Fate of other Evangelists and Apostles—James in Jerusalem, and John in Asia Minor—External Boundaries of the Church at the Death of the Apostle John.

THE day of Pentecost marks the beginning of the independent Apostolic regulation of the visible Kingdom of Christ. Next to the time of its original foundation by Christ himself, it is the most important era in the history of the Church; for now-first it fully displayed in public its distinctive character. Hitherto it had been partially obscured; for the time of its manifestation had not arrived. Christ was first to be crucified, and his successor, the Spirit, to be sent from heaven, before the external organization of the Church was to be brought prominently into view. Before this, indeed, the Apostles had initiated into it by baptism, and had preached of its' establishment; but they had done so under the personal supervision of Jesus; and they had, besides, introduced a few of the Jews alone into the Christian community,—and of these, only those who were most susceptible of religious instruction and enlightenment. Now, a new era had begun,—the era of the Spirit's influence,—in which the Church was to array herself in beautiful garments, to go forth in all her majesty among both Jews and Gentiles, and, ultimately, to bring the world into subjection to her sway.

The miraculous manifestations attending the outpouring of the Spirit upon the assembled disciples, on the day of Pentecost, excited astonishment throughout all Jerusalem. To the wondering multitude which had flocked to the place where the disciples had met together, Peter proclaimed the Gospel; and, at the conclusion of his discourse, "they that gladly received his word, were baptized; and the same day there were added (to the Church) [* Our received version of the New Testament has here in Acts 2: 41, "added *unto them*"; the ellipsis occurring in the Greek being supplied by "*unto them,*" i. e. the Apostles, or the disciples. The connection of the sentence, however, and a comparison with verse 47 below, will show that the ellipsis should be filled up, as we have filled it, by the words *to the church* De Wette, in his admirable version of the New Testament, renders, in accordance with this view, by 'wurden *zu der Gemeinde hinzugefugt;*" and with his rendering corresponds that of others of the best among modern interpreters)].about three thousand souls" (Acts 2: 41),—the first fruits of the Apostolic harvest, the first persons who became Baptists under the special dispensation of the Spirit.

From this time forth the Church increased in numbers and in power; but, for some years, its influence was confined chiefly to the city of Jerusalem, which the Apostles had constituted the centre of their operations. On the death of Stephen, the deacon, however,—which occurred probably in the year 36 A. D., from three to five years after the memorable day of Pentecost,—the disciples, being persecuted, were scattered abroad throughout Judea and Samaria; and "they went everywhere",—at length, even into Syria, and to the island of Cyprus,—"preaching the word". The Apostles, however, still remained in Jerusalem.

Philip, one of the seven deacons of the church in Jerusalem, laid the foundation of a community of believers in Samaria; and, by baptizing the eunuch, was probably the means of founding a church in Ethiopia. He preached the Gospel, moreover, in the towns situated on the sea-coast of Palestine; and finally took up his abode in Cæsarea, as the founder, probably, of a church in that city. His labors in Samaria were confirmed and prosecuted still further by Peter and John; and, on the Palestinian sea-coast, by Peter.

Paul, miraculously converted not long after Stephen's death,—perhaps in 37 A. D.,—having spent three years in Damascus and in Arabia, returned, through Jerusalem and Cæsarea, to his native city Tarsus; in which, no doubt, as well as in other cities of Cilicia, he proclaimed the Gospel.—Before his conversion, the "Apostle of the Gentiles",—then called Saul,?"made havoc of the church" which was at Jerusalem; and was the chief actor in the "great persecution" which scattered abroad all the disciples "except the Apostles". When "the blood of the martyr Stephen was shed," he stood by and approved the execution. But the life of Stephen was not sacrificed in vain. The persecution which commenced with his martyrdom, was the means of sending the Gospel out of Jerusalem; and of establishing churches in Judea and Samaria, and, ultimately, among the Gentiles of Asia Minor and Europe. Saul himself, who "was consenting unto his death," was brought, by a special interposition of Providence, to a knowledge of the truth; and straightway, after his baptism in Damascus, "he preached Christ in the synagogues, that he is the Son of God."

Meanwhile, the first Gentile converts, Cornelius the centurion, and a number of his kinsmen and friends, were baptized by Peter; when he saw "that on the Gentiles also was poured out the gift of. the Holy Ghost" (Acts 1.0: 45); and thus was laid the foundation of the Church among the Gentiles.—Soon after, tidings having come up to Jerusalem, that a number of the Greek Gentiles in Antioch had "believed and turned to the Lord," Barnabas, a Hellenist by birth, and a prophet and teacher in the church at Jerusalem, was sent forth to this Syrian city, to instruct and regulate the infant community which had been established there by disciples,—by birth "men of Cyprus and Cyrene,"—who had been driven forth from Jerusalem upon "the persecution that arose about Stephen". He and Paul,—whom Barnabas had brought from Tarsus,—for a whole year (43-4 A. D.), "assembled themselves with the church, and taught much people" in Antioch,—the city where the disciples were first called "Christians".

In the meantime, in the year 44, persecution broke out afresh and more violently against the Church in Jerusalem. Herod Agrippa laid violent hands on the Apostles. James "the elder", the son of Zebedee, was put to death; and Peter was saved from a similar fate only by a miracle. Though Herod died the same year, Jerusalem ceased from this time to be the secure seat of the Apostles. The "Acts of the Apostles" from this point, is almost wholly occupied with a narrative of the several missionary journeys of Paul, and the establishment of the Church, through his own and the labors of his converts and assistants, in the principal cities of the Gentiles, in Asia Minor, and the southern part of Europe. These journeys of the great Apostle, as related by Luke, were three in number; the first commencing in the year 45, and the last terminating in 58; when, on his going up for the fifth time to Jerusalem, he was arrested and sent a prisoner to Cæsarea. Thence, two years afterwards, he was taken a captive to Rome; and here the narrative of Luke, the author of the "Acts of the Apostles", leaves him in the third year of his captivity (62 A. D.).

The New Testament gives us very little further information respecting the subsequent movements and fate of the Apostles and their disciples. Still, however, we are not left altogether in the dark; for other writings lend us at least a feeble light.

Respecting Paul, Clement of Rome (†100), his contemporary and his disciple, speaks in a manner that implies, and justifies us, perhaps, in inferring, his release from the imprisonment mentioned by Luke, and his martyrdom, at a subsequent period, in Rome (cp. 2 Tim. 4: 6-9). His disciples, particularly Silas, Timothy, and Titus, continued to carry out his principles and plans after his death. Peter,—spoken of for the last time in the New Testament as being in Babylon (probably in 64 A. D.),—according to later, but not altogether conclusive, testimony, came, at length, to Rome, and there suffered martyrdom in company with Paul (67 A. D.), in the reign of the monster Nero. Mark, who was with Peter in Babylon, founded, it is thought, the church in Alexandria, in Egypt. Timothy is said to have been martyred in Ephesus, under Domitian, or Nero; and Titus to have died in Crete. Thomas, according to ancient traditions, preached the Gospel in Parthia; Andrew, in Scythia; Bartholomew, in India; and Philip, who survived all the apostles but John, in Hierapolis and Phrygia.

James, "the Lord's brother",—who, both before and after the death of Paul and Peter, was the head of the church in Jerusalem, with an apostolic authority,—suffered martyrdom in that city, in 69 A. D., the year before its destruction.—About the same time, or not long before, John,—now, perhaps, the only surviving apostle,—repaired to Asia Minor; and there, or in the isle of Patmos, composed, in the year 69, the Apocalypse, or book of Revelation. Here, in Asia Minor, with Ephesus as the central-point of his operations, this Apostle, according to ancient and quite reliable traditions, clearly traceable to his immediate disciples, lived and labored till the close of the first century. For thirty years he remained in this region; visiting the Christians in the country adjacent; organizing churches, and superintending them with apostolic power and authority. His spirit was infused, into and long pervaded the churches of Asia Minor; the deep traces of his ministry continuing plainly visible far down into the second century. In the year 100, John died; and with him closes the Apostolic Age of the Christian Church.

The preaching of the early Christians,—of the disciples in general, as well as of the Apostles,—spread a knowledge of the Gospel, before the close of the Apostolic Age, into nearly every country then belonging to the Roman Empire; and in various parts of the Roman dominions,—particularly in the cities situated in that portion of them now known as the Empire of Turkey,—a number of churches was established. Not a few of these are mentioned in the writings of the New Testament; chiefly, however, those which were founded during the life, and by means, directly or indirectly, of the missionary labors of "the great Apostle of the Gentiles". Many other communities, besides those expressly mentioned in the New Testament, were established through the agency of the Apostles and of the disciples at large; but within what geographical boundaries, and in what numbers, cannot now be precisely determined. Clement of Rome (†100), who was contemporary with the Apostles, and was, perhaps, the same Clement spoken of by Paul in his letter to the church in Philippi (4: 3), says, in his first Epistle to the Corinthians (§5) that Paul proclaimed the Gospel "both in the east and in the west"; that he "taught righteousness to *the whole world"*; and that "he came to *the boundary of the west"*, in the prosecution of his missionary enterprise. If these expressions of Clement's are not to be regarded as rhetorical, they would seem to intimate that Paul, after his release from his first imprisonment, preached the Gospel to the westward of Rome. Ancient tradition asserts that he traveled into Spain; and it is not improbable that he did so. Spain, perhaps, really heard and obeyed the voice of the Apostle; but the claims of Britain to an apostolic origin for its churches,—based by some on the passage in Clement referred to,—are much more doubtful. That country, as well as France and Germany, may have heard, but seems not to have received, the Gospel, until early in the second century.

§2

Qualifications for Admission—The Visible Church Catholic—Meaning of the word "Ecclesia"—Individual, or Single, Churches—Character and Duties of the Membership—Independence of the Single Churches—Church Officers: Presbyters (Elders), Deacons, Deaconesses—Their Duties and Powers—Consecration to their Office—Office of the President, Presiding Presbyter, or Bishop, at the Close of the First Century—Support of the Church Officers—Completion of Church Organization at the End of the Apostolic Age.

THE Church of Christ, as founded by himself, and as fully established, after his death, by the Apostles, was a visible community of baptized believers in Christ Jesus as the Messiah. It had but two sacred rites: ***Baptism,*** which was an ordinance initiating into its membership; and the ***Lord's Supper,*** which was commemorative of the life, sufferings, and death of its divine Founder. Jesus himself established these two rites for his Church in all time; and these, it has been well said, "it is not lawful either to ***change*** or to abrogate".—The qualifications for admission into this visible community, this "communion of the saints", were, simply, repentance of sin, and belief in the Messiahship of Jesus; for, in this age, "whoever professed to regard Jesus Christ as the Saviour of the world, and to depend on him alone for salvation, was immediately baptized," and made thereby a member of the Church.

Though truly one and visible, the Church was not an organic unity in the generally received sense of that expression; not a great ecclesiastical organization, fashioned after the model of a civil corporation. It was a unit, as being , "the body of Christ": it was a unit, as having "one Lord, one Faith, one Baptism"; and it was a unit, as forming an external opposition to the unbelieving, and as having an external centre-point in the Apostles, who exercised a general supervision over all the single churches of which the entire visible body, the Church Catholic[3], was composed, and were co-presbyters in every single community. Beyond this supervision of the Apostles, however, there existed, during the Apostolic Age, no external bond of union holding together the various communities, or single churches, into which the Church as a whole was divided.

The Church was, from the necessity of the case, composed of and represented by a number of separate communities, or individual churches. These possessed in common the ordinances of the Church Catholic; and the members of each were, as to all essential qualifications, members of the others. As members of *the* Church, *all* believers were bound, by virtue of its missionary constitution, to make known the Gospel everywhere, by word and by deed. As members of *a* church, a branch of the whole body, they were to meet together at stated times, for public worship, for instruction and edification in matters pertaining to religion, and for the celebration of the ordinance of the Lord's Supper.—The Church, as such, was essentially a missionary organization; and all its members, *without exception,* were mouthpieces for the proclamation of the glad tidings of salvation throughout the world. The churches, as such, were religious societies, in which and by which the ordinances were to be preserved; and through whose agency, by means of its duly appointed teachers, a knowledge of religious truth was to be kept alive, and to be propagated and increased, as far as possible, by suitable training and by proper discipline, among the membership. The object of the Church was the conversion of the world to Christ: the object of the churches was the religious training of those who were already believers, and their better preparation for the life to come.

As believers in Christ, and as members of his Church, the brethren are called,

---

3 The expression "the Church Catholic", is not found in the New Testament. It occurs first in the Epistle of Ignatius (†116) to the church in Smyrna (§8); where it is said, "Wherever Christ is, there is *the Catholic Church"*. The expression is equivalent in meaning to "the Church Universal," i.e. "the Community of the Saints", considered as one body. In this sense it is used here, and elsewhere, in this hook. It has no reference, of course, to the ecclesiastical organization known as the (Roman) Catholic Church.

in opposition to "the world", "*the Saints*", "*the Elect*", "the Called",—a people chosen by and dedicated to God. In these appellations, however, "there was no claim to moral perfection, but a remembrance of their high calling in Christ"; for, even in this period, under the very eyes of the Apostles, many found admittance to the Church who had undergone no real transformation in their moral character; and to whom, as individuals, the appellation "Saints" could not with propriety have been applied.

In that early age, the distinction which sometimes has to be made in our day between Christians and church members, had not, and could not have, arisen. All who had, on profession of repentance and faith, received baptism, were constituted, by the act, members of the Church; and they alone of all men bore the name of "Christians". Something more, therefore, than belief in Christ, was necessary to constitute one a Christian: there was required also a formal incorporation into his body, the Church, by the voluntary reception of the ordinance of baptism. "Believers", "Saints", "Brethren", "the Elect", "the Household of Faith", "Christians", were terms synonymous and convertible. Each designated those, and *none but those,* who, having professed faith in Jesus as the Messiah, had, by baptism, been made members of his body, the Church Catholic and Apostolic.

The Greek word usually translated *Church* occurs one hundred and fifteen times in the New Testament; in which it refers, in one hundred and ten instances, to the New Testament dispensation in one or another of its aspects. If we except the instance of its occurrence in Heb. 12: 23 (in which the sense of the word is doubtful) and 1 Cor. 11: 18 (where the word signifies *an assembly*), the term means, in all these cases, either 1., *A church,* that is, a *church individual,* or *congregation* of believers residing, or assembling, in a particular place; or 2. THE *Church,* that is, *the Church Catholic or Universal.*

By "Church Universal" we mean the whole visible community of Christian Believers, constituting, in several important senses, a distinct Society. This "Church Universal" is the entire visible body of Christians,—that community which Christ founded upon earth; in which he established ordinances to be perpetuated through all time; over which he appointed the Apostles rulers; and against which, he promised, the gates of hell shall never prevail. It is a spiritual kingdom; a commonwealth separate from all earthly commonwealths and governments; an organization distinct from every other, more glorious than all, and destined, at last, to conquer and subdue all. Such is "the Church" spoken of in Matt. 16: 18. Such, too, is "the Church" as represented frequently in the Epistles of Paul (e. g. Rom. 16: 23; 1 Cor. 10: 32; Gal.l: 3, 13; Eph. 1: 22, 3: 10). In a word, such is "the Church" every where in the New Testament, with a few (perhaps *four*) exceptions, wherever the word does not refer to a particular society residing, or meeting, in a particular place.

Some writers on Church Polity deny that the term *ecclesia* ever means the "Church Universal", as above defined; and contend that the word, when it does not signify "a particular local society of Christians", designates "the whole body of God's redeemed people",—"all, on earth and in heaven, who are-members of Christ, united by faith to the living head". According to this view, *ecclesia,* when it does not designate *a particular church,* refers always to (what is sometimes called) *the "Church Invisible,"*—the whole body of true believers in heaven and on earth, out of whose communion there is no salvation. The idea of an "Invisible Church" as so conceived, is not indeed foreign to the New Testament; but this idea is never, strictly speaking, denoted in the New Testament by the term *ecclesia.* That word,—it will be found on a careful examination of the sixteen or seventeen New Testament passages in which it refers to the Church Universal,—bears only that sense which we have assigned it.

It is no valid objection to the view which we advocate, that the "Church Universal" is sometimes spoken of as composed of "saints", "the elect of God"; and that other predicates indicative of holiness and perfection, are applied to it by the New Testament writers. In cases of this kind, much is very properly predicated of the Visible Church which in strictness is applicable only to the Invisible; it being *taken for granted,* that, in the case of every professed believer, the outward profession of faith has a corresponding inward reality. In such instances, the New Testament writers do not mean to assert, or even to intimate, that every professed believer to whom or of whom they speak, is truly a "saint," or truly one "of the elect of God": they only refer to the *idea* of membership in the visible body of Christ; according to which idea, membership is presupposed to be, though in many cases it may not be really, based upon an actual spiritual communion, by regeneration and adoption, with Christ, the living head of the Church.

Ecclesia (from *ekhaleo, to call out, to summon*) means, originally, not so much a *congregation,* as a *convocation,* that is an assembly which has been convoked. As applied to the Church Universal, therefore, it signifies *the convocation* (an expression analogous to "*the elect*", and equal to *the divinely-called body*) *of all those who profess faith in Christ.* This idea, then, of the Church Universal, is, perhaps, more native to the word,—more conformable to its original signification,—than that of a *particular church, or congregation*[4].

The first single church established among the Jews was that of Jerusalem; according to the model of which the other churches subsequently formed among the Jewish people for the most part conformed. Among the Gentiles, the first church was established in Antioch; and this,—modeled upon that in Jerusalem, which latter was itself a model, in some respects of the Jewish synagogue,—formed, in general, the pattern of those afterwards founded among the Gentiles.

Each church was an independent body; and no one was subject to the control or jurisdiction of another. Those communities which had been founded by the Apostles in person,—particularly the church in Jerusalem (cp. Acts 15),—were frequently consulted on doubtful points of ecclesiastical regulation, or on cases of church order; but "they had", as Mosheim declares, "no judicial authority, no control, no power of giving laws". This power resided only in Christ and in his representatives, the Apostles. "On the contrary", continues the same historian, "it is clear as the noonday that all Christian churches had *equal rights,* and were, in all respects, on a footing of equality. Nor does there appear, in this first century, any vestige of that *consociation* of the churches of the same province, which gave rise to ecclesiastical councils and to metropolitans," Yet were the churches connected together by a common bond; and that bond was the College of the Apostles.

Among the members of each church there was, at first, if we except the Apostles, no peculiar and consecrated class, possessing powers and privileges which the

4   Since the above was written, the Author of this book has received a work, lately published, entitled "*Christ Our Life*", and written by the Rev. Dr. Angus, an eminent English Baptist scholar and divine; in which he finds, much to his gratification, that President Angus holds substantially the same theory as is here advocated, respecting the Church Visible and the relation to it of churches individual or particular

other members did not enjoy. They recognized each other as brethren and sisters; and among the membership there existed perfect equality. After a time, however, as necessity demanded and good order required, each church had its regular Officers, by whom its affairs were regulated and administered; and these possessed a positive and well-defined official authority.

These Officers were; first, the Presbyters of each community, sometimes also called ***Bishops.*** The term ***Elder*** is equivalent to ***Presbyter.*** There were originally, it is probable, several Presbyters, or Elders, in each church; who were officially of equal rank; but in many churches, particularly towards the close of the Apostolic age, individuals among them,—as James in Jerusalem,—obtained, on account of superior piety or wisdom, something of a personal authority over the others. The duty of the Presbyters was, in general, to attend to the ***religious*** affairs of the community. The second class of church Officers were the ***Deacons,*** or ***Ministers,*** and, in many churches, the ***Deaconesses;*** who were under the superintendence of the Presbyters. Their business was, in general, to transact the ***temporal*** affairs of the community.

That there were ***Deaconesses*** in the Apostolic churches, both the New Testament and all ecclesiastical antiquity testify. In Rom. 16: 1, Phœbe is spoken of as "a ***servant*** of the church in Cenchrea; where the words "a ***servant***" should be rendered "a ***deaconess***" (***diaconon***). In 1 Tim. 3: 11, ***deaconesses*** are no doubt referred to; certainly, not ***the wives of the deacons,*** as the received English version represents.—The other two passages of the New Testament (Phil. 4: 3; 1 Tim. 5: 9-10). sometimes cited as referring to ***deaconesses,*** cannot be relied on for proof. The more important of the two, 1 Tim. 5: 9-10, is descriptive, most probably, of ***female presbyters.*** Pliny the younger (†110), in his letter to Trajan, speaks of women who held the office of the deaconship, describing two of them as "ancillæ quæ ministroe (***female ministers***) dicebantur."

The Deaconesses had charge of the sick; and attended, in particular, on the women, at their baptism, etc. By means of them, "the Gospel", Neander well remarks, "might be brought into the inmost recesses of family life; where from Eastern manners, no man could have obtained admittance."

At first, in the newly planted churches, the officers, especially the Presbyters, were appointed by the Apostles; always, however, at the nomination, or at least with the consent, of the churches themselves. Afterwards, they were appointed, if not by an Apostle, by an apostolic assistant,—such for example as the "evangelists" Timothy and Titus,—the whole church consenting; or they were nominated, as Clement of Rome testifies, by the leading men of the church, and then elected by the free suffrages of all the people.

After being appointed, church Officers were formally inducted into office by the ceremony of ***imposition of hands,*** performed either by an Apostle, by an assistant of an Apostle or an Evangelist, or by the Presbytery (or College of Elders) belonging to the Church,—according as the case or the occasion required.—By means of the same ceremony, the laying on of hands (***cheirothesia***), others besides these regular church officers were consecrated, in those times, to the work to which they had been regularly set apart. In this way, too, were the special powers of the Spirit conferred upon Christians at large; and in this way were the "evangelists" solemnly consecrated to their missionary labors.

Towards the close of the century, as the churches became larger, and the number of Presbyters increased, it appears to have become the practice among them to appoint, or in some way to recognize, one of their number as their ***President*** (the ***proestos*** of Justin Martyr), and as the central-point, or representative head, of the whole society. Such a position James the Just, "the brother of the Lord", held in Jerusalem; and, after his martyrdom (69 A. D.), Symeon (†107), who is also reputed to have been a relative of Jesus. This officer is the person alluded to under the title "***angel***" in the Apocalypse; afterwards styled, in all churches, ***the bishop.*** He was not, however, a bishop in the modern sense of that term; for, as Mosheim correctly remarks, "he had charge of a ***single*** church, which might ordinarily be contained in a private house; nor was he its ***lord,*** but was in reality its ***minister*** or servant; he instructed the people, conducted all parts of public worship, and attended on the sick and necessitous, in person; and what he was unable thus to perform, he committed to the care of the presbyters; but without power to ordain or determine anything, except with the concurrence of the presbyters and the brotherhood."

All these officers,—the Presbyters, the Deacons, and, at a later period, the Bishop,—as well as the poor of the church, received their support, so far as they needed it, from the free-will contributions, or ***oblations,*** of the brotherhood; and from these free-will offerings, moreover, were drawn supplies "for the public exigencies and for unforeseen emergencies". The people, therefore, still preserved, and sometimes, when occasion demanded, exercised, the ultimate and supreme power in the regulation of the affairs of the churches; "for they also", as Mosheim says, "by their suffrages rejected or confirmed the laws, that were proposed by their rulers in their assemblies; they excluded profligate and lapsed brethren, and restored them; they decided the controversies and disputes that arose; they heard and determined the causes of presbyters and deacons; in a word, the people did everything that is proper for those in whom the ***supreme power*** is vested."

A complete and permanent organization of the Christian congregation, or church individual, was not, it is important to remember, effected at once by the Apostles. We find in the Gospels no account whatever of church organization; and the fragmentary notices contained in the "Acts of the Apostles",—found especially in the first part of that book,—relate, for the most part, to a provisional and imperfect organization. During this period, special reliance was placed upon personal Apostolic guidance, and upon the ***charisms,*** or spiritual gifts, possessed by individual Christians in that age of the Church. By degrees, however, and as necessity or convenience required, "well-defined and permanent offices were introduced",—as Dr. B. Sears correctly states in his published Address on an "Educated Ministry",—"till, at length, near the close of the Apostolic times, we find a few offices recognized in all the churches, quite irrespective of extraordinary or miraculous gifts."—Only here, then, in the closing period of the Apostolic era, do we find certain examples of permanent church Officers; and now only do we reach the time in which the organization of the churches was brought to its completion.

§3. CHURCH USAGES AND PRACTICES.

Regular Times for Public Worship—Places of Holding Assemblies—"House-Churches"—Their Connection with the City Church—The Order of Religious Exercises in the Assemblies—Prof. Jacobi on the Mode of Church Worship—Hymnology of the Early Church—The Recognized Teachers of the Church—Each Church the Judge of Admission to its Fellowship—The Discipline of Immoral Members.

THE members of each church assembled for public worship, and for religious edification, on the first day of every week; which was called "the Lord's Day", because on it Christ rose from the dead; and this was done by Apostolic precept and example. Some churches,—composed wholly or in part of Jews,—observed also the seventh day of the week, or the Jewish Sabbath, as a day not to be devoted to the ordinary avocations of life. Such retained also the Jewish festivals in general; and it is not improbable that even the Gentile Christians, towards the close of this period, regularly observed the Passover, or Easter, as the anniversary of Christ's sufferings and death.

The places of assembling were usually rooms in the private dwelling-houses of Christians; which, from being given-up to devotional purposes, became in a sense consecrated and holy, as apartments dedicated to the worship of God. In some of the larger cities, on account of the number of members, the churches were divided into several smaller communities, holding their meetings in different places.

The **house-churches** spoken of in the New Testament (Rom. 16: 5, Col. 4: 15, Philem. v. 2), are examples of these "smaller communities". "Whether they had each an independent government, or were branches, or "arms", of the city churches, cannot, perhaps, be determined with entire certainty. They might have had each their special Elders, and yet have been branches of the main city community. Those passages in the New Testament in which the collected Elders of one city are represented as acting as a whole (Acts 15: 4, 20: 17. coll. Phil. 1: 1, Jas. v. 14), speak, as Gieseler truthfully says, "for the connection of the Elders of one city into a College, and, consequently, of the churches in houses into one church".—Dr. J. L. Reynolds, in his "Church Polity" (p. 53), inclines to this latter view; and thinks that it "is rendered probable by the existence of a plurality of bishops" in some of the leading cities.

It is possible, however, that these house-churches were not under a common government; and that in those passages where a number of Elders is mentioned as being in one city, "each governed independently a particular church". Supposing this to be the correct view, it may be inferred, with a good show of reason, that every church, in Apostolic times, had but **one** Elder, and not a **plurality,** as the analogy of the synagogue would indicate, and as most ecclesiastical historians maintain. The question, "What was the connection between these **house-churches** and **the city church,**" needs, from Baptists, a more full and thorough investigation than it has yet received.

In the public assemblies of the church, there took place an interchange of reading out of the Old Testament and explanation of what was read. With this was connected, in some congregations, the reading of Apostolic Epistles; not yet, however, of the Gospels,—for of these there existed as yet no universally received collection; while those which were received were employed only in private use, and not in the churches. To reading of the Old Testament Scriptures there succeeded, at first, in all congregations, free religious discourse and exhortation, singing and prayer. After these exercises, there usually followed the administration of the Lord's Supper, of which only the initiated, or members of the church, were allowed to partake, "The other regulations of the churches", Gieseler correctly remarks, "were left free to each society, innocent national customs being observed; and therefore they differed in separate communities."

The mode of conducting Public Worship", says Prof. J. L. Jacobi, in substance, in his Church History[5], "was a free imitation of the worship of the Jewish synagogue. Portions of the Old Testament were read; perhaps in a regular order, to supply at the same time the want which could not be supplied by private reading. Soon such Apostolic Epistles as were directed to the whole congregation, were accustomed to be read (Col. 4: 16, 1 Thess. 5: 27); and, at a later period the Gospels. Exposition and hortatory application were added to the reading. Other discourses, spoken in a somewhat free manner by those endowed with the *charisms* [i. e., special gifts of the Holy Spirit] of teaching and prophecy, were, on occasions, delivered in the Christian assembly. Speaking-with-tongues, which manifested itself in a way quite peculiar, was made to contribute by interpreters to the general edification. The offering of prayer was in part the regular duty of the leader (or pastor); and it was left partly to the free promptings of each one's pious feelings. The singing was inartificial; and was struck up sometimes by individuals (1 Cor. 14: 26), and sometimes by all the assembly (Col. 3: 16). In singing, the Psalms of the Old Testament were chiefly employed; but in connection with their use we find the germ of a Christian poetry proper (1 Cor. 14: 26; Eph. 5: 19)."?Thus far Jacobi on the mode of conducting Church Worship in the early part of the Apostolic Age of the Church.

---

5 Lehrbuch der Kirchengeschichte, erster Theil (1st Vol.), p. 67.—This volume treats of Church History down to 590 A. D.—A promised English translation has not yet, it seems, appeared.

Our information respecting the hymnology of the Apostolic Church, and of the early Christians in general, is extremely scanty. The most distinct notice of it which we have, is that in Pliny's Letter to Trajan (written about 110 A. D.), in which he says that the Christians in their assemblies were wont "to sing a hymn in alternating strains [secum invicem] to Christ as God".—Paul exhorts the brethren in Ephesus and those in Colosse to admonish one another "in psalms, and hymns, and spiritual songs". If these expressions refer to different kinds of singing, then we are probably to understand by "psalms" the Psalms of the Old Testament; by "hymns and spiritual songs", the free devout effusions which were prompted by the Spirit in minds susceptible of such kinds of composition. This singing of the early Church seems to have taken upon itself a recitative form (*cantillation*); and thus singing and prayer were not so diverse as they are in our day.

Originally, any one who felt impelled by the Spirit, was allowed to speak and to teach in the Christian assembly; every believer being, in one sense, a priest and anointed of the Lord. "When, however, the spirit of prophecy and the *charismata* (spiritual gifts) died away, this privilege was confined chiefly to the bishop and presbyters, whose peculiar office it was,—in addition to regulating the order of the church,—to give instruction in the doctrines and duties of Christianity. The special guidance of the Spirit being withdrawn, good order required that the office of instructing the church should be limited to those who were "apt to teach". The Epistles to Timothy and Titus show that, near the close of Paul's life and labors, only those who possessed the requisite qualifications, and not the members indiscriminately, were allowed to rule and to give instruction in the churches.—Women were suffered to take no part whatever either in the public instruction or in the government of the churches; not being permitted even so much as "to speak in the church" (1 Cor. 14: 34, 35; 1 Tim. 2: 11, 12).

Every Christian community possessed the right of determining whom it would, and whom it would not, receive into its immediate fellowship. Baptism initiated into the Church Catholic; but admission into a church individual was obtained only by the voluntary consent of its membership.

As each community had the right to receive into its fellowship, so it possessed the right to exclude a member from its communion. In the exercise of this right,—in some cases, this solemn duty,—the churches excluded immoral members (1 Cor.

5: 2–13); and restored them only on condition of repentance and amendment (2 Cor. 2: 5–8). The fundamental principles of discipline adopted by each community, are laid down in Matt. 18: 15–18.

§4. THE ORDINANCE OF BAPTISM.

The Initiatory Rite of the Christian Church—Its Nature as an Outward Act, and its Essential Idea—The Recipient's Confession of Faith—The Administration of the Ordinance—The Apostolic Baptismal Assistants—Baptism "out of the Church"—Proof that Immersion alone is the Apostolic Ordinance—Baptismal Formula in the name of the Trinity—The German Philologists on "Baptizo"—Dr. Robinson's Definition of the Term—The "Notion" of some American Pædo-baptists—Objection of Dr. Robinson on the Score of "Scarcity of Water", Shown to be Untenable—Number and Capacity of the Pools of Jerusalem, and of Palestine.

The distinguishing rite of Christianity is ***Baptism;*** for it initiates its recipient into the Church, the visible community of Christian believers. Whenever spoken of in the New Testament, or in other written records belonging to the first century, the ordinance is represented as the ***Immersion in water of a Believer in Christ, in the name of the Father, Son, and Holy Spirit, or in the name of Jesus.*** Its essential idea is entrance into communion with Christ; and by its reception believers are united to the visible body of the Lord, and received into the communion of the redeemed, the Church of Christ (1 Cor. 12: 13, Gal. 3: 27). Not only, therefore, does it initiate its recipient into the Church; it is also a symbol of his regeneration, of his being born again; of his participation in the divine life of Christ, and in the promises which are grounded upon the atonement; and of his spiritual union with the other members of the Church of Christ.

The ordinance was administered to a believer upon a profession of repentance for sin and of faith in Jesus of Nazareth as the Christ; and it is quite probable that, even in this Apostolic period, particularly towards its close, a brief verbal confession of belief in Jesus as the Redeemer was publicly made by the candidate just before his reception of the ordinance.—Such a practice seems to be alluded to in 1 Pet. 3: 21, in the words "***the answer*** of a good conscience toward God", which may refer to replies given to questions proposed by the administrator to the believer at baptism.

"At first", as Mosheim declares, "all who engaged in propagating Christianity, administered this rite"; and whoever was the instrument of converting a person, he also could confer upon him the ordinance of baptism. When, however, a number of individual churches had been constituted, and when it became necessary that some established order should be followed, the right to baptize,—as also the right to administer the communion, or Lord's Supper,—was restricted, it would seem, to the **bishops,** or **presidents,** of the churches, and to persons who had received ordination in the character of evangelists. The precise time of this change is not readily determined; but the usage appears to have been well understood and followed in the latter part of the first and early in the second century.—The same rule is established, for the sake of good order, in the Baptist churches of the present day; but it is also understood and admitted by them, that, in cases of necessity, baptism may be validly and properly administered by one who has not received ministerial ordination.

The Apostles seem to have baptized not so much with their own hands as by assistants. In the case of Cornelius and his friends, Peter "***commanded*** them to be baptized" (Acts 10: 48); and Paul baptized personally only a few of the members of the church in Corinth (1 Cor. 1: 14-16). The latter named Apostle thought it of little importance to perform the baptismal ceremony with his own hands; and deemed his office as preacher a more worthy one than his office as baptizer (v. 17). He does not intend, however, by the remark "God sent me not to baptize, but to preach the Gospel," to disparage the baptismal ceremony; for his conduct during his whole ministry and his language in his Epistles, show that he considered no one a member of the visible Church, until he had been baptized into its communion. Paul could not have meant to undervalue the rite itself; since the obligation to receive baptism is as strong and as binding on the believer, as his previous obligation to exercise repentance and faith.

Those assistants of the Apostles who administered baptism in their stead, may, or may not, have been ordained ministers. They must, however, have been themselves members of the Church; for there is no hint in all the New Testament, or in any writings of the Apostolic Age, that any person, himself unbaptized, ever performed the baptismal ceremony. It is inconceivable that such a thing should have occurred; it being manifest that no one can initiate into a society of which he is not himself a member. To suppose the contrary, is to suppose an absurdity.

Hence those Baptists are correct, who contend that baptism performed "out of the church" (***extra Ecclesiam***) is not Christian baptism at all; and they do right in insisting, as they do, that those who,—supposing themselves already baptized, because ***immersed,***—present themselves for membership in their churches, should,—if immersed by one not himself baptized,—receive the true and valid baptismal consecration, before they can be admitted into church fellowship. "Before they can be admitted into ***church*** fellowship", we say, not "***Christian*** fellowship": since, into the former, none but the baptized can be received; but into the latter, all who believe in and love the Lord Jesus Christ may be, and ought to be, admitted, without questioning and without hesitation.

That ***Immersion*** alone was considered Baptism in the Apostolic Age, is proved by several considerations.—1. It is clear from the ordinary meaning of the Greek term which designates the ordinance; for the word, both in that and in every previous and subsequent age of Greek literature and usage, means, when employed literally, immersion and immersion alone; and so the entire Greek church, so called; has practised to the present day.—2. It is proved also by the circumstances attending the instances of baptism mentioned in the New Testament; many of which circumstances can consist with no other idea than that the candidates were immersed, while none are irreconcilable with that supposition.—3. It is proved, finally, by the symbolical import attributed to the rite by Paul; who represents it to be an emblem of the death, burial, and resurrection of Christ, and of a moral participation in these and their benefits on the part of the recipient. This it could not be. if the ordinance were anything else than immersion.—These considerations have settled, in the minds of the most distinguished biblical scholars, of every name and religious sect, the important question, mooted still in some quarters, as to what was the nature of Christian baptism, in the Apostolic period, as an outward act; and this they all, with singular unanimity, acknowledge to be ***an immersion*** into water in the name of the Trinity, or in the name of Christ Jesus.

It must be admitted, that it can not be proved that our Lord meant to establish an invariable baptismal ***formula,*** when he commanded the Apostles to baptize "in the name of the Father, and of the Son, and of the Holy Ghost". Several passages in Acts (as 2: 38; 8: 16; 10: 48; 19: 5) show that the rite may be properly, and perhaps in

Apostolic practice was not unfrequently, administered in the name simply of Christ Jesus. Baptism in his name alone, is, if rightly understood, baptism in the name of the Trinity.—The regular formula was prevalent in the time of Justin Martyr (†166). It afterward became universal; and some churches of a subsequent period even went so far as to declare that no other baptism was *valid* but that which was administered in the name of the Trinity.

The German philologists, biblical and classical, almost without exception, assign to the Greek verb *baptizo* the signification to *immerse;* and do not admit even *to wash,*—much less *to pour upon,* and still less *to sprinkle,*—to be, properly speaking, a meaning of the term, Their opinion on this point controls that of the learned world; even those scholars who practice the contrary in ecclesiastical usage, admitting the philological fact, while practically denying its legitimate inference.

An eminent biblical lexicographer of America, however, the learned Pædo-baptist Dr. Edward Robinson, contends, in the late edition of his New Testament Lexicon (1850), that *baptizo,* though meaning, as he admits, only to *immerse,* "in Greek writers from Plato downwards, would seem to have expressed in Hellenistic usage, not always simply *immersion,* but the more general idea of *ablution* or *affusion".* The proofs brought forward by him to sustain this position, are singularly weak and infelicitous. Their total inadequacy to establish what Dr. Robinson desires, is strikingly pointed out by Prof. H. J. Ripley, in his "Remarks on Dr. Robinson's Lexicon".

The attempt of a number of American and English Pædo-baptist writers,—men, generally, "of little Latin and less Greek",—to show that *baptizo,* in biblical usage, means not only *to dip,* but also *to pour upon,* and even *to sprinkle,*—that is, *to apply water sacramentally in any way,*—is hardly worthy of notice; for it conflicts not only with the results obtained by the careful and unprejudiced investigations of every An eminent biblical lexicographer and philologist of the present day, but with the simplest and most elementary rules of verbal interpretation.— The still more untenable opinion, that the Greek verb, as used in the New Testament, "*never* means *to immerse,* but always *to pour upon* or *sprinkle",*—a notion which is so ludicrous that it could hardly have arisen, or could scarcely be entertained seriously, anywhere but among the most prejudiced of the Pædo-baptists in

America,—is so manifestly absurd, that one wonders how any man could be found who would waste his paper and ink in advocating the idea, or his time in reading a treatise that defends it.

The opponents of Immersion as alone Baptism, see a difficulty,—"apparently insuperable" in their estimation,—in the way of a total immersion, on account of the supposed scarcity of water conveniences for the rite in Palestine; but especially in the city of Jerusalem, where, "in Acts 2: 41 three thousand persons are said to have been baptized, apparently in one day, at the season of Pentecost in June." So the case is put by Dr. Robin-son, in his New Testament Lexicon.

The chief objection on the score of scarcity of water has reference to Jerusalem; in which, however, as also in other parts of Palestine, it can be, and has been, shown, by proofs irrefragable, that sufficient, nay abundant, water conveniences for the performance of baptism must have existed. The results of recent researches in Jerusalem,—even those made by Dr. Robinson himself,?"can hardly fail",—as Dr. Ripley says in his "Remarks",—"to produce conviction that a city, so wonderful for the labor and skill expended in securing immense quantities of water for both public and private use, could not have been destitute of places in which baptism, immersion we mean, could have been administered to an indefinite number of persons.?When we read of remains of ancient reservoirs, in length 316 feet, in breadth from 200 to 218 feet, and 18 feet in depth; also, in length 592 feet, in breadth from 245 to 275 feet, and in depth from 35 to 42 feet; and when various notices of aqueducts and other means of supply pass before our minds, showing great ampleness of accommodations for water, and a most remarkable attention to the safety and comfort of the city in every vicissitude of circumstances, it does seem utterly unreasonable to cast suspicion on the meaning of the word *baptize* by the suggestion that the city could not supply a sufficient quantity of water for immersing so many as the inspired account may warrant us in saying were baptized."[6]

Besides those conveniences for immersion which are common, even at this day, in most cities and towns of the East, Jerusalem possessed, in Apostolic times, special facilities for the performance of the Christian ordinance, in the large public *pools* and *fountains* of the city. Of these, *six* are worthy of particular notice:—1. *The*

---

6 Rev. Prof. H. J. Ripley, in his "Remarks on Dr. Robinson's Lexicon", published in the "Baptismal Tracts for the Times" (Boston, 1861), pp. 100, 101.

pool of Bethesda —360 feet long, 130 feet wide, and 75 deep, which is at this time "partly filled with rubbish".—2. *The pool of the King, or of Solomon,* —which even now furnishes "an abundant supply of water, and also (if needed) retirement even for change of raiment".—3 *The pool of Siloam,*—53 feet long, 18 broad, and 19 feet deep; on the bottom of which stands at all times two or three feet of water, but any required depth "may be readily obtained by damming temporarily the mouth of the outlet".—4, *The Old Pool,* or *the Upper Pool in the highway of the Fuller's Field,*—316 feet in length, 218 broad at one end and 200 at the other, and 18 feet deep; a "broad basin of water which could hardly have been better adapted to immersion, if it had been (specially) constructed for that purpose".—5. *The pool of Hezekiah,*—240 feet long, and 144 wide; "furnishing even now an ample supply of water for bathing at the season of the ancient Pentecost", and possessing, as did all the deep pools of Jerusalem, "every facility for a gradual descent into the water"; and which is still used for bathing purposes.—6. *The lower pool of Gihon,*?a *pond* 592 feet long, from 245 to 275 feet broad, and from 35 to 42 feet deep; a reservoir now dry, but as late as the time of the Crusaders, "so abundantly supplied with water that all the city were allowed to use it freely; and it was the great watering-place for horses". This reservoir has sides with "a slope just adapted to a descent for immersion"; and it contains" ample room for all the seventy, and for the twelve added, to act as administrators of the sacred rite" on the day of Pentecost.   Such were the principal pools of the metropolis. Palestine at large, besides the river Jordan,— which is distant about fifteen miles from Jerusalem,—and various smaller streams or brooks, possessed numerous pools and fountains in which immersion could have been, and doubtless often was, performed in the days of Christ and the Apostles. Of this no proof needs to be adduced in the present connection[7].

---

7   For the valuable information above given, respecting the Pools of Jerusalem, and for the quotations, we are indebted to a very timely and learned treatise of 50 pages, written by the Rev. G. W. Samson, of Washington, D. C., who has himself travelled and made observations in Palestine. It is published in the "Baptismal Tracts for the Times," under the title "The Sufficiency of Water for Baptism at Jerusalem, and elsewhere in Palestine, as recorded in the New Testament". It is a most satisfactory and conclusive reply to the objections of Dr. Robinson

§5

Believers alone Subjects of the Baptismal Ordinance in this Age—The Baptism of "Households" no ground for inferring the Existence of Infant Baptism—Proofs, independent of New Testament Positive Testimony, that the Rite was now Unknown—Passages of the New Testament sometimes adduced in its Favor, given up by all the Leading Biblical Critics and Philologists—The Doctrine that Infant Baptism is recognized in the New Testament, "not tenable at the Bar of Biblical Criticism."

The *Subjects* of Baptism throughout the Apostolic Age, were believers in Christ, and believers alone. The pre-requisites to the reception of the ordinance,—repentance and faith,—exclude by implication, as the Apostolic commission (Matt. 28: 19) does expressly, all who are not capable of intelligent action. Accordingly, there is found in this period, either in the New Testament, or in the written memorials now extant, no example of the baptism of any but believers.

Some have supposed that the *households* whose baptism is mentioned in the New Testament, included infants; and that upon these also the baptismal rite was performed. This supposition, however, cannot be true; for in these instances of household baptism, the recipients of the ordinance are also spoken of, in nearly every instance, as doing other acts which intelligent and reasoning beings can alone perform. And, even if there had been infants in some or in all of these households, and even if faith and other acts implying intelligence had not been, as they are in nearly every case, predicated of the households, there would still be no just ground for inferring that the infants were baptized; since, from the very nature of the case,?baptism being consequent only upon faith,—they would have been excluded from the reception of the ordinance.

All those passages of the New Testament, therefore, which are cited by Pædo-baptist controversialists,—chiefly, now-a-days, in America,—in proof that infant baptism was in use in Apostolic times, and is even recognized in the New Testament, form no substantial ground-work for an historical argument in favor of the practice as apostolic in origin or authority. There can be no reasonable doubt, that the eminent Pædo-baptist theologian Schleiermacher was right,, when he said, "All traces of infant baptism which one will find in the New Testament, *must first be put into it"*; and with his decision that of all the biblical scholars of Germany,?and of all the unprejudiced biblical critics of England and America, who have thoroughly studied the subject,—is, if not in form, at least in substance, altogether coincident.

In addition to the New Testament positive historical and exegetical proof against Infant Baptism in the Apostolic Age, its non-existence is rendered probable, if not absolutely certain, by the following considerations:—1. On the supposition that the practice was known in the time of the Apostles, cases of it must have frequently occurred; yet not an instance of it is adduced in the New Testament; while, on the other hand, the baptism of adults is frequently mentioned.—2. An instance of a baptism without previous instruction and faith in the Gospel, is not recorded in the Scriptures.—3. Had the practice been in existence, Paul could not have done otherwise than allude to it, when treating, as he often does, of the rite of circumcision.—4. The early and long-continued opposition manifested to the baptism of children in the ancient Church,—an opposition which forms the subject of the most ancient passage in any of the Fathers (Tertullian) in which the rite is mentioned,—would be inexplicable, had the ordinance been then considered unquestionably an Apostolic institution.

"The opinion," therefore,—we may conclude in the words of Dr. Hackett,—" that Infant Baptism has any legitimate sanction", either directly or by implication, "from any passage in the New Testament, is no longer a tenable opinion at the bar of Biblical Criticism" It is a misapplication of the ordinance of baptism, altogether unknown in the days of the Apostles; and belongs not to Apostolic Christianity.

The passages of the New Testament chiefly relied on to prove the "apostolicity" of Infant Baptism, are Acts 16: 15, 18: 8, and 1 Cor. 1: 16; but these passages when tried by the test of criticism, utterly fail. They have been surrendered without reserve by the leading biblical scholars of Europe,—men whose ecclesiastical relations would naturally lead them to a different conclusion; who belong to Pædo-baptist churches; and themselves practice infant baptism as an appropriate Christian ceremony, though freely acknowledging, at the same time, that the usage has no warrant from scriptural precept and example. Among these scholars are such German theologians, historiographers, and philologists, as Neander, Olshausen, Jacobi, Hagenbach, Meyer, De Wette, Rückert, Augusti, Gieseler, Guericke, Engelhardt, Tholuck, Hahn, Lange, Knapp, Münscher, Neudecker, Couard, Rössiler,

Starck, Höfflmg, etc.,—men who, it may be remarked, hold also to the Baptist view that immersion was in Apostolic times alone considered Christian baptism.

Against the united testimony of such scholars, and many others of like learning,—critics of very different mental tendencies and characteristics,—no opinion on a biblical question can readily stand. "We may safely decide therefore, with Prof. H. B. Hackett[8], that" no decision in biblical criticism not absolutely unanimous, can be considered as better established at the present time, than the utter insufficiency" of the New Testament passages referred to in support of Infant Baptism to prove, or in any way to justify, that practice "as an Apostolic institution".

§6. THE EFFECT AND IMPORT OF BAPTISM.

The Direct Effect of Baptism—The Ordinance Symbolical in its Import—A Sign of "the Remission of Sins"; and a Symbol of the Moral Purification of its Recipient—The Outward Rite Spoken of, metonymically, as though an Agent in the Remission of Sins—The New Testament Passages supposed to teach "Baptismal Regeneration"—View of Prof. H. J. Ripley—Brief History of the Doctrine of "Baptismal Regeneration"—The Doctrine in Modern Times.

Baptism, as we have seen, initiates into the visible Christian Church. This is its only direct effect as an operative agent; and thus much it does for every one that receives it, whether he he truly converted or not. It is a divine institution; the heaven-appointed means of an outward acknowledgment of Jesus Christ, and of the renunciation of "the world, the flesh, and the devil"; and, therefore, the public badge of Christian disciple-ship. Its reception is enjoined upon all believers as solemnly and as formally as repentance and faith are commanded. It was necessary that Christianity should possess some distinctive outward initiatory ceremony; and the head of the Church determined that this initiatory rite should be *Immersion.* He chose Immersion, it would seem, on account of its peculiar significance. What that significance is, we call the *design,* or *import,* of Baptism.

As instituted by our Lord, Baptism was a *symbolical ordinance,*—a symbol of the *regeneration,* the *new spiritual birth,* of its recipient. It *signified* that the sins of the candidate had been forgiven; that he had been cleansed and purified from iniquity, through the meritorious atonement of the Lord Jesus Christ; and this

---

8   "Tracts for the Times," already quoted, p. 167

idea of moral purification was most beautifully symbolized, or typified, by the total immersion of the candidate beneath the baptismal waters. The external rite was merely an immersion into water, an outward washing of the body from impurity; possessing itself no saving efficacy, and indicating "the remission of sins" only so far as it was truly significant of an inward purification, and a faithful representation of the spiritual regeneration of its recipient. That which the ordinance symbolized, was the element in it the reception of which was essential to salvation,—*the new birth from heaven,* produced by the operation of the Holy Spirit.

Baptism, then, symbolized the moral purification of him upon whom it was conferred; and so it is represented, metonymically, by Paul in Eph. 5: 25, 26, and in Titus 3:5; and in particular, by John in John 3: 5, and by Peter in 1 Peter 3: 21. Such was the divinely-intended import of the rite; but it has also other related significances; the chief of which have already been mentioned. Thus, for example, the ordinance is spoken of by Paul as emblematic of the death, burial, and resurrection of Christ; and as in this way emblematic also of the candidate's death to sin and resurrection to a new life of righteousness and holiness (Rom. 6: 2–4). And this is thought by some to be what the rite was originally and solely designed to symbolize; an opinion manifestly not in harmony with the complete Scriptural representation.

Symbolizing, as it did, the moral purification of its recipient, Baptism is sometimes, for the sake of brevity, spoken of in the New Testament, by a common figure of speech,—the use of the sign for the thing signified,—as a direct operative agent in the remission of sins (John 3: 5; Acts 2: 38; 22: 16; Eph. 5: 26; Titus 3: 5; 1 Peter 3: 21). Such a metonymical employment of language is quite common in the Scriptures, as it is in other writings of the East. The members of the church in Corinth, for example, are addressed by Paul as persons who have been "washed", "sanctified," "justified" (1 Cor. 6: 11); and yet not a few of them had evidently, according to the Apostle's own judgment, never been truly regenerated by the Spirit of God. In like manner, the membership of other churches is assumed, in other passages of the New Testament, to be connected by a living union with Christ; when, in point of fact, a number of its constituents had never been really converted to the truth (Gal. 1: 6; 4: 21; Rev. 2: 15, 20; 3: 16).

So, with regard to Baptism, regeneration is presupposed in the case of all its recipients, unless the contrary be expressly stated or clearly implied; and, on this account, the term "Baptism," which literally designates only the external rite, is sometimes, for the sake of brevity or convenience, used by the New Testament writers, by the rhetorical figure called synecdoche (taking a part for the whole), to represent a more complex idea,—an idea which comprehends not the outward ordinance merely, but also the moral spiritual purification which that act symbolizes. Thus intimately related, by a blending as it were of type and antitype, the external ceremony and the internal regeneration are sometimes represented by the sacred writers as though one and the same,—that efficacy being apparently ascribed to the outward, which has been, and can be, wrought only by the inward. This complex idea, this complex reality, is Christian Baptism in its highest sense; and this is the only baptism that has anything to do with the external, which has the power to effect regeneration.

In three of those six New Testament passages in which the efficacy of Baptism seems, to some minds, to be ascribed directly to the external rite, the writers appear to have carefully guarded against a possible misconception of their meaning; the true idea being elucidated by the addition of a qualifying clause or circumstance. Thus, in Titus 3: 5, we find the qualifying circumstance, "***and renewing of the Holy Ghost***" (if we have here a true rendering, which is disputed); in John 3: 5, the additional and qualifying idea, "***and*** of the Spirit",—"except a man be born of water ***and of the Spirit";*** and, in particular, in 1 Pet. 3: 21, an important qualifying addition; where we are expressly told that "the putting away of the filth of the flesh" (the mere outward ceremony of immersion) does not save the recipient of the baptismal ordinance, "but the answer of a good conscience toward God",—an honest profession of the truth, based upon a correct knowledge of Jesus as the Son of God and the mediator of the New Covenant.

In harmony with this view, and confirmatory of it, are the following remarks on Acts 22: 16,—a passage which is one of the strongest proof-texts of the advocates of baptismal regeneration—taken from the excellent popular Commentary on the "Acts, of-the Apostles" of the Rev. Dr. H. J. Ripley, Professor in the Newton Baptist Theological Seminary: "The Gospel regards all men as sinners, needing not only forgiveness, but also the purifying of their hearts from sin. This purity of heart, produced by the Holy Spirit's influence, and a reception of Christ as the crucified and risen Saviour, is emblematically signified by the ordinance of baptism in the purifying element of water. Hence a believer in Christ, when receiving baptism, may justly be said, in a figure, to be washing away his sins; as he is, by that ordinance, showing externally what has been commenced in his soul, and is manifesting his serious purpose, through divine influences, perpetually to cultivate holiness of heart and life.—Baptism is the external public entrance on the Christian life; so that the Christian may be said at his baptism to lay aside his sins, to cleanse himself from moral defilement, and to commence a new life. As the body is made clean by water, so the soul is cleansed by divine grace; and what is thus inwardly performed, is outwardly expressed by this significant emblem. It was customary, also, in the first years of the Gospel, for some external token to be granted from above at the administration of baptism, as showing God's approval of the act, and acceptance of the persons; and thus the finishing evidence of pardon and of acknowledged discipleship was bestowed in connection with baptism; so that that ordinance was eminently a washing away of the person's sins. The external token to which reference is made, was the imparting of special gifts by which God manifested his approbation of the Saviour's followers, and fitted them for giving effectual testimony to the Gospel. And not unfrequently, in every succeeding age, has it been the case, that the reception of baptism has been honored by the Lord, as the occasion of a peculiar manifestation to the soul of his pardoning mercy and sanctifying power."

Baptism, therefore, was, in the Apostolic Age, a symbol of the moral purification of its recipient,—a figurative washing away of the sins of every candidate upon whom it was performed. Whenever that which was symbolized by the outward act, corresponded with the inward reality,—whenever, that is, the sin-remitting "baptism of the Holy Spirit", whether bestowed previously to, or simultaneously with, the external bodily immersion, accompanied the outward and visible ordinance,—then and there occurred an instance of Christian baptism in its highest and most significant sense. Such a baptism,—and this is a conception not foreign to the New Testament,—was not only a *symbol* of the internal moral purification of him that received it; but, it may also be said, a *seal* and solemn proof to him, that his sins had been remitted through his faith in the blood of the Redeemer.

That baptism is represented in the New Testament as in some way connected with "the remission of sins," cannot be doubted by any one who has read the Scriptural record with an attentive and unprejudiced mind. In what manner, and to what extent, it is so connected we have endeavored above to determine. In some of the passages which have been examined, the baptismal rite, seems, as we have seen, to be represented as itself the direct operative agent in the remission of sins. It appears contrary to reason, however, and not consonant with the New Testament idea respecting the spiritual nature of the kingdom of God, to suppose that any merely external rite can confer forgiveness. Yet many have so believed; and that from an early period in the history of Christianity.

The doctrine of "baptismal regeneration," in one or another of its various forms, is probably as old as the most ancient of the so-called "Apostolic Fathers"; some of whom lived in the latter part of the Apostolic age of the church. The dogma is quite distinctly brought forward in the "Epistle" of Barnabas; which, even if not written by Barnabas (so often mentioned in Acts) himself, was certainly composed somewhere in the beginning of the second century. It is unquestionably taught in the "Shepherd" of Hermas; a book composed, if not by Hermas, by some Christian of the latter part of the first or early part of the second century. Justin Martyr († 168) undoubtedly teaches the doctrine; and so do Clement of Alexandria, Irenæus and Tertullian.

None of these writers hold, if rightly interpreted, that the waters of baptism are, in and of themselves, efficacious to the cleansing away of sin; but rather that regeneration is, according to divine appointment, conferred by the Holy Spirit simultaneously with the outward act of immersion. At a later period, however,—after that, in accordance with the teachings of Origen and Cyprian, the rite of baptism came to be considered the universal remedy for original sin, and to be conferred even without a previous exercise of faith on the part of its recipient, in order to wash away this original corruption,—the doctrine that the mere outward ceremony produces remission of sins, in and of itself, regardless of the mental condition of the candidate, became quite prevalent in the Christian world. So teach the Romanists at the present day, and so their Church has officially taught since the year 1311, in conformity with the decree of Pope Clement V., passed in the Council of Vienna. This dogma is put forth in its baldest form by Cardinal Bellarmine, a distinguished Roman Catholic writer, who was a member of the Council of Trent; and the Roman Catechism, composed by the decree of the same Council (1566), gives a view almost entirely coincident with that of Bellarmine. The same doctrine is now held by the high-church Episcopalians.

The dogma of baptismal regeneration is incorporated, moreover, in one form or another, into most of the principal Protestant Confessions of Faith; the Confession of Augsburg (1530), the Swiss Confession (1536), the Genevan Catechism (1545), the Confession of the Church of Scotland (1560), the Confession of the Reformed Churches of France (1561), the Articles of the Church of England, (1562), the Heidelberg Catechism (1563), etc.

This doctrine is also the distinctive tenet of the "Disciples" of the present day; but in what precise sense it is so, it is rather difficult to determine. There seems to be among them no fixed and settled view on this point; some of their writers explain the doctrine in one way, and others in another. Their head and most distinguished leader, Mr. Alex. Campbell, appears to have himself materially modified, of late, his former published opinions on this subject. In his last work on "Christian Baptism" (1851), he describes the ordinance as "a symbol of moral purification,—a washing away of sin in a figure, declarative of a true and real remission of sin,?*a formal and definite release of the conscience from the feeling of guilt and all its condemnatory power"* (p. 258). In another passage, he says that the rite is "in one point of view, a *sign* of the burial and resurrection of the Lord Jesus, and of our burial and resurrection in and with him; and, in another point of view, a *seal* of the righteousness of faith, or the remission of all our past sins, through faith in his blood, then, and in that act, publicly expressed and confirmed" (p. 272).

These expressions, however they may be interpreted, do not, it must be admitted, teach baptismal regeneration in the same sense in which it seems to have been formerly advocated by Mr. Campbell; and certainly not in the sense in which it is held and proclaimed by some of his followers. The doctrine, as he now explains it, is not as strongly put as it is in the Articles of the Church of England (Art. XXVII). It is substantially the same as that taught in the (Presbyterian) Westminster Catechism and Confession of Faith (1643); nor is it very materially different, as far as we can see, from the view given in the orthodox Baptist Confession of Faith,—published, originally, by the Baptists of Great Britain in 1689, (itself modelled after the Westminster Confession), and adopted by the Philadelphia Association in 1742. That standard Confession defines the ordinance in the following terms (Ans. to Quest.

97): "Baptism is an ordinance of the New Testament, instituted by Jesus Christ, to be unto the party baptized a sign of his fellowship with him, in his death, and burial, and resurrection; of his being ingrafted into him; of remission of sins; and of his giving himself up unto God, through Jesus Christ, to live and walk in newness of life."

§7. ORDINANCE OF THE LORD'S SUPPER.

Import of, and Time of Receiving, the Lord's Supper—Its Original Character, and mode of Administration—The Recipients of the Ordinance—The Unbaptized not Subjects of Communion—Recapitulation of Results—The Primitive Church essentially Baptist in its Usages and Ordinances.

The *Lord's Supper,* though an ordinance of the Church Catholic,—belonging, like baptism, to the original plan of its divine Founder,—can, from the nature of the case, be celebrated only by individual churches. The ordinance, as instituted by Christ, was simply commemorative of his life, sufferings, and, in particular, his death; and so only it was understood by the first Christians. Wherever, in primitive times, there was a congregation of believers assembling regularly on the Lord's Day,—and, at first, even more frequently,—there the Eucharist was accustomed to be celebrated. The bread and wine for the Supper were taken from the offerings of the brotherhood. The elements, after being blessed by the president or pastor of the church, were distributed to the assembled believers by the deacons.

Originally, the Eucharist was connected with the *Agape,*—a social supper partaken of by the faithful, whenever they assembled; and, it would seem, the ordinance itself partook, at first, in no small measure, of the character of an actual evening meal. If Justin Martyr's "Apology" to Antoninus Pius,—written, it is quite certain, not later than 139, A. D., be good authority for this century also, the elements of the Supper were not only partaken of by the believers who were present in the assembly, but were sent also, through the deacons, to those who were absent from the meeting. Of this Supper no excluded member of a church was allowed to partake, nor indeed to participate in any of the church exercises; until he had, after due repentance, been restored to fellowship. Each church was the sole judge as to what particular persons should be admitted to its communion.

The Load's Supper can be administered only to those who have been baptized;

and it is not proper for any others to partake of the ordinance. This relative order of Baptism and the Eucharist, has been followed from the earliest period of Christianity; and it is that which every denomination of Christians still upholds, as well in practice as in theory.—The corruption of the rite of Baptism among Pædo-baptists, however, has led to a practical difficulty respecting inter-communion, in the Lord's Supper, between them and those who hold to the sentiments of the Baptists. Those who think that only believers' immersion is valid baptism, cannot, it is evident, consistently practice church communion with those who have not been immersed. To do so, would be to break down the visible partition-wall between the baptized and the unbaptized,—between members of the Church and non-members; and this they can not, conscientiously and consistently, do. Baptists, therefore, as a general rule, hold, now-a-days,—and hold very properly,?to non-communion in a church relation with the members of Pædo-baptist communities.

The history of the Church of Christ, in its outward development, in its constitution, and in its usages and ordinances, has now been traced, briefly but minutely, from its foundation by our Lord until the death of its last Apostolic lawgiver. The period has been reached in which its organization was complete; when, at length, it stood forth a glorious and perfect Church, "built upon the foundation of the Apostles and Prophets, Jesus Christ himself being the chief corner-stone" (Eph. 2: 20).

It has been shown, in the course of our examination, that the Church was composed of members who, on a credible profession of faith in Jesus as the Messiah, had been initiated into it by baptism; that those who belonged to it had duties as members of the Church Catholic and as members of a church individual,—duties distinct and yet united; that the single churches were independent of each other, and were presided over by officers of their own appointment, or selection; that each church made provision for regular public worship, and for the religious and moral instruction and discipline of its membership; and that every church observed two sacred rites, instituted by Christ himself,—Baptism, which, as the initiatory rite of the Church Catholic, was preliminary to membership in a church individual; and the Lord's Supper, which, though an ordinance of the Church Catholic, was, from the nature of the case, celebrated only by churches individual.—It has been shown, furthermore, that Baptism was, during this period, immersion, and only immersion; and that Infants were not considered entitled to the ordinance, and never, therefore, received it in Apostolic times.—It has been shown, finally, that Baptism was a symbolical rite, possessing in and of itself no saving efficacy, but was significant of a higher spiritual baptism which does confer the forgiveness of sins; and that the Lord's Supper, being a church ordinance, was not administered to any but church members, and, consequently, only to those who by baptism had outwardly put on Christ.

Such were the principles and practices of the Church in the Age of the Apostles,—from the Ascension of our Lord to the death of the Apostle John. Are not the views and usages, it may now be asked, of those known among Christians as the Baptists, substantially, and in all essential points, identical with the doctrines and usages of Christianity during this Apostolic period of the Church of Christ? And, may we not say of them, as said the great Hebrew lexicographer and biblical critic Dr. William Gesenius, when he heard described the principles and practices of the English Baptists, "*Why, how exactly like the primitive Christians!*"—It is indeed true: the Baptists of the present day are, and the Baptists of all times have been, "like the primitive Christians". They are substantially like them in their church constitution; and precisely like them in their mode of observing the ordinances of the Church,—ordinances of which one at least, the initiatory rite of the Church, has been perverted, among all other Christians, either from its original form or from its original and true intention. The Baptist model is the Apostolic model; and, so far as they conform to this, so far they are built upon a foundation which can never be overturned.

And not only is the Baptist Church of modern times *like* the Primitive Church; it is the *same* Church, come down through the long lapse of ages, amid opposition and persecution, uncorrupted in its doctrine and pure in its ordinances. "*The Baptists*",—it is candidly and honestly said by two distinguished Pædo-baptist scholars of Holland,?"*may be considered as the only Christian community which has stood since the days of the Apostles; and as a Christian Society which has preserved pure the doctrines of the Gospel through all ages.* The perfectly correct external and internal economy of the Baptist denomination, tends to confirm the truth, disputed by the Romish Church, that the Reformation brought about in the sixteenth century, was in the highest degree necessary; and, at the same time, goes to refute

the erroneous notion of the Catholics that their communion is the most ancient".[9]
So testify the Lutheran Drs. Ypeig and Dermont; and their testimony is true. The
"Baptist communion" is indeed "the most ancient" in the world; for, reaching back,
it connects itself by many a bright link with the communion of the Church Apostolic and Universal. In a word, it is the Church of the Apostolic Age budding forth
into new life, and destined to fill the whole earth with its branches.

CHAPTER III.
THE AGE OF THE "APOSTOLIC FATHERS" AND OF THE FIRST "CHRISTIAN FATHERS": FROM THE DEATH OF JOHN TO THE RISE OF AFFUSION AS BAPTISM AND OF INFANT BAPTISM, 100—250 A. D.

§1. EXTERNAL DEVELOPMENT AND PROGRESS OF THE CHURCH.

Different Periods of the Apostolic Age—The Closing Period—John in Ephesus—Churches under Apostolic Disciples—The "Apostolic Fathers" of Paul's
School—The "Apostolic Fathers" of the School of John—Brief Account of the Writings of the Six "Apostolic Fathers",—Barnabas, Clement, Hermas, Ignatius, Papias,
and Polycarp—The First "Christian Fathers",—Justin, Irenæus, Tertullian, Clement
of Alexandria, Hippolytus, Cyprian, and Origen—Progress of the Church among
the Jews—Progress among the Gentiles in the East and in the West—The Gospel in
France, Germany, and Britain—The Founders of the British Churches—Christianity in Britain at the End of this Period.

THE Apostolic Age of the Church closes with the end of the first century, the
year of the death of the Apostle John. This Apostolic era has naturally three divi-
sions; the first extending from "the day of Pentecost" probably of 31 A. D. (our Lord
having most likely begun his public ministry in the year 781 of Rome, that is, in 28

---

9   This testimony is given by Dr. Ypeig, Prof, of Theology in the University of
Groningen, and Dr. J. J. Dermont, Chaplain to the King of Holland, in a Treatise of
theirs entitled "Origin of the Dutch Baptists". The volume was written for the use
of the Government; and was published in 1819, at Breda. The authors were both
members of the Dutch Reformed Church; and, being Pædo-baptists, would not,
without a clear conviction, have testified in favor of the Baptists.

A. D.) to the conversion of the Apostle Paul (about 37 A. D.); the second, from the conversion of Paul to his martyrdom in 67 A. D.; the third, from the martyrdom of Paul to the death of the Apostle John, 100 A. D. During the last thirty years of the Apostolic age, therefore, only one Apostle out of the whole number,—if we except Philip, who is said to have been yet surviving during the first part of this period, laboring in Hierapolis of Phrygia,—was still alive and engaged in the work of propagating the divine principles of Christianity. After the destruction of Jerusalem (70 A. D.) that Apostle made Ephesus,—the capital of Ionia, and, during the Roman dominion, the capital and most prominent city of Asia Minor also,—the central-point of his operations; and this city, together with Antioch, in Syria, continued, in consequence, long to be the centre of Christianity in Asia Minor, and in the East.

The churches of this region, therefore, still enjoyed, during the latter part of the first century, the privilege of an apostolic superintendence; of which the Christian communities in other regions had for some years been deprived. Here John laid broad the foundation of the Church, by his preaching, and, in particular, by giving special instruction to able disciples and by his apostolic writings; while the churches of other prominent cities, both in and out of Asia Minor, were under the guidance, for the most part, of trustworthy persons who had been immediate disciples of an Apostle. Of these Apostolic disciples but little, and much of that little doubtful, information has come down to our day. The only ones truly known to modern times are the three most ancient of the six Fathers who are called, by way of eminence, "Apostolic"; a few written productions of whom are still extant. They were developed in the school of Paul; and were all, perhaps, his personal disciples. These three are the following: ***Barnabas,***—possibly the same so often mentioned in Acts,—from whom we have an Epistle yet in existence; ***Clement,*** bishop of Rome (cp. Phil. 4: 3),—who died in the same year as John,—whose "Epistle to the Corinthians" is of historical importance; and ***Hermas*** (cp. Rom. 16: 14), whose "Pastor" (***Shepherd***) was composed, most probably, somewhere between the beginning and the middle of the second century.

On the death of John the last Apostle had been summoned from the earth, and the Church was deprived forever of direct Apostolic guidance; but there still lived men, formed under John's spiritual training, under whom in particular, in connection with other teachers, its instruction and government still continued. Of these, those who are known to us through their writings are the remaining three of the "Apostolic Fathers"; whose influence, while living and when dead, was long felt in the churches of Asia Minor and the East, and, in respect to one of them, has not, as regards church organization, ceased operating to the present day. They flourished during the first part of the second century; and, having long testified to the truth of Christianity, sealed their testimony with their blood. These three are the following: *Ignatius* (†116), bishop of Antioch, in Syria, from whom we have seven Epistles,—genuine, but perhaps interpolated,—of considerable value from their bearing on the disputed question respecting the nature of church organization in the latter part of the first and the former part of the second century; *Papias* (†163), bishop of Hierapolis, in Phrygia, of whose writings only fragments remain; and *Polycarp* (†167), bishop of Smyrna, in Ionia, from whom there is extant an Epistle, most probably genuine, to the Philippians.

As these six "Apostolic Fathers" form the connecting link in the Church between the teachers of Apostolic times and of the important era immediately succeeding,—the age, namely, of the Christian Fathers,—it is necessary that every one who desires to become acquainted with the progress and development of the Church, should know all that can be ascertained respecting the writings which they have left to the world. A brief account is here subjoined, as essential to a thorough understanding of the history of the Church during this transition period from apostolic to non-apostolic direction and control.

THE SCHOOL OF PAUL.—The *"Epistle"* of *Barnabas* is first mentioned by Clement of Alexandria (†220). It consists of twenty-one chapters; the first seventeen of which treat "of the abrogation of the Mosaic dispensation, and of the types and prophecies relating to Christ"; while the last four are made up of practical directions and exhortations. Critical opinions are quite equally divided in our day as to the genuineness of the Epistle. Rosenmüller, Bleek, Gieseler, affirm; Hug, Neander, Winer, Hefele, deny. The external evidence is in favor of its authenticity: the internal seems to be against it. The chief ground urged against its genuineness, is its mystical mode of interpretation. According to the Epistle's own representation, it was written soon after the destruction of Jerusalem. Even if not the production of the Barnabas of Acts, the Epistle was certainly composed as early as the first part of the second century.

The *"Epistle to the Corinthians"* by *Clement* was usually read in the meetings of the church at Corinth as early as the second century. It is admitted on all hands to be genuine; but certain portions are thought by a number of critics to be interpolated. The Epistle was written not later than 100 A. D., the year in which Clement suffered martyrdom under Trajan, in Rome. Some authorities (as Wotton, the publisher of the most correct text of the Epistle, and Hefele) date its composition as far back as 68 A. D. It was, however, probably written in 96 or 97, at the close of the persecution under Domitian. The object of the Epistle was to quiet dissensions which had arisen in the church at Corinth; and to repress exhibitions of insubordination on the part of certain persons in the church toward its presbyters. In tone and spirit, and in justness and soberness of thought, it approaches nearer to the apostolic writings than any other production of the "Apostolic Fathers". A *second* Epistle attributed to Clement, is undoubtedly spurious; and the "Apostolic Constitutions", the "Apostolic Canons", the "Recognitions of Clement", and the "Clementina", also attributed at one time to this Father,—are unquestionably suppositious, and belong to a later period in church history.

The *"Pastor"* of *Hermas* is mentioned as early as the time of Irenæus (†202), who even speaks of it as "Scripture". It is frequently quoted by Clemens Alexandrinus, and by Origen (†254). We possess, except a few fragments of the original Greek, only a Latin version of the work, which, however, is as old as the time of Tertullian (†220). Modern Editors have divided it into three Books; "the first consisting of four Visions, the second of twelve Commands, and the third of ten Similitudes". The *Shepherd* "inculcates moral precepts in visions and parables, in order to promote the completeness of the Church". If written by the Hermas of Paul, the work was composed, probably, in the latter part of the first century: if written by another person, it is a production of not later than the first part of the second century.

THE DISCIPLES OF JOHN.—The seven *"Epistles"* of *Ignatius* were written on his journey from Antioch to Rome, whither he was going to die as a martyr to the cause of Christianity. They are directed, respectively, to the churches of Ephesus, Magnesia, Trallis, Rome, Philadelphia, Smyrna, and to his friend Polycarp of Smyrna. They have come down to us in two recensions, a longer and a shorter; of which the latter is now generally admitted to be the original. The fact that the dignity and powers of Bishops are exalted higher in these Epistles than in any other writings of this age, has made their genuineness the subject of sharp contention and controversy. The settled opinion now is, that the shorter recension is authentic; but that the text needs correction,—some passages in the Epistles bearing strong marks of having been introduced by another and a later hand than that of Ignatius. Eight other "Epistles" attributed to this same author, are unquestionably spurious.

Papias wrote five Books, consisting of traditional accounts of Christ, of the Apostles, and of other early Christian disciples. He is represented by Eusebius as having advocated a "gross millennarianism in his writings".

The "*Epistle to the Philippians*", by *Polycarp,* is mentioned by Irenæus, who, it seems, was well acquainted with Polycarp; and he speaks also of Epistles sent by him to the neighboring churches. It is divided into 14 sections; of which the first nine and the thirteenth exist in the original Greek, the others only in an ancient Latin version. The genuineness of the Epistle is called in question by many; but it is probably authentic. Polycarp himself was burned alive in 167,—Marcus Aurelius reigning in Rome,—at Smyrna, in the 86th year of his age. The encyclical Epistle descriptive of his martyrdom, written by the church in Smyrna, is still extant, in two recensions. It is not without its value.

As the teachers who had been trained under direct Apostolic guidance, disappeared, one after another, from the Church, others were prepared,—some under their immediate influence, and some with an independent development,—to fill the vacancies made by their death in the ranks of Christian instructors. The most distinguished of these,—those who possessed the most reputation in their own day in the churches, by whom especially the churches were moulded in doctrine and in discipline, and whose influence is still potent among many Christians,—were *Justin, the Martyr* (†166); Irenœus (†202), a scholar of Polycarp's, and bishop of Lyons, in France, about 177 A. D.; *Tertullian* (†220), educated a lawyer, but, after his conversion, a presbyter in the church at Carthage, in North Africa; *Clement, of Alexandria* (†about 220), a presbyter of the church in that city; *Hippolytus,* who was a pupil of Irenæus, lived about 225 A. D., and was, probably, bishop in Portus, at the mouth of the river Tiber, in Italy; *Cyprian* (†258), bishop of Carthage; and, above all, *Origen* (†254), a pupil of Clement of Alexandria, and a scientific theologian,—the most eminent and the most learned, though not always the most safe, Christian scholar and instructor of his age.

The first mentioned of these teachers,—all of whom are ranked among the "Christian Fathers",—*Justin Martyr,* as he is usually called, was educated a philosopher. He was born of Greek parents, about 89 A. D., in Samaria. After his conversion,—which was effected by his study of the Scriptures,—he resided for the most part in Rome, in the character of a Christian philosopher; and there he devoted himself to the furtherance of the truths of the Gospel. After the Apostles, he was the 'first, in order of time, of learned Christian divines. Martyred at Rome in 166 A. D., he left, besides other works, two "*Apologies*", or defences of Christianity,—the longer written about the year 139, the shorter about 166,—which, as showing the more important usages and doctrines of the Church in his time, are invaluable to the ecclesiastical historian. They form the chief connecting link between the books of the New Testament and the writings of the Church Fathers of the second and third centuries of Christianity.

It would be well, could a sketch of the writings and history of these first Christian Fathers be given in this connection; but the limits assigned to this volume forbid the attempt, however brief. Their written productions, suffice it to say, not only moulded, in a great degree, the doctrines and usages of the Church during the age in which they lived, and wrote, and labored, and also during subsequent periods; but they are still regarded by a large number of professed Christians as the standard of theological appeal, and the safest and most reliable interpreters of Scripture.— Chrysostom and Augustine, of the following period, only carried out,—the one in the East, the other in the West,—the logically-developed ideas and principles which these Fathers had laid down in their theological treatises[10].

During the period now under consideration,?from the year 100 to the year 250,—the Church, persecuted though it was, by the permission and sometimes at the order of the Roman Emperors, made no little progress among the Gentiles both

---

10   As regards *Cyprian,* Rev. E. J. Shepherd, of England, has, in a late work on the -History of the Church of Rome, denied the genuineness of the writings attributed to him; and he even contends that Cyprian himself is "probably an imaginary personage". Could these assertions be substantiated, something would be gained on the Baptist side of the baptismal controversy; but the proofs which Mr. Shepherd adduces in favor of either position, are critically speaking, decidedly unsatisfactory.

of the East and of the West. Among the Jews, however, it had rather become an object of hatred and aversion; and the people among whom it had been founded, and from whom it had received its first members, became now, and continued to be from this time forth, as far as their power permitted, its bitterest persecutors. After Jerusalem was sacked in the year 70, the church in that city ceased to be "a model mother-church, and the centre of Christendom". The church in Ephesus took its place as the model and head of the Christian communities. The members of the church in Jerusalem, as temporarily restored, were hated by their Jewish countrymen even more cordially than before, and were persecuted by them yet more relentlessly; for, after the destruction of the capital city of the Jews, the dividing line between Judaism and Christianity was necessarily drawn more closely than ever before.—After the final overthrow of Jerusalem and the complete desolation of Palestine, in the reign of Hadrian (135), the inhabitants of the metropolis and the Hebrews in general were scattered abroad into every land; and Christianity, henceforth, could only now and then gain a convert from among the Jewish people. The work of conversion, therefore, was, during this period, limited, for the most part, to the Gentile world.

In the East, as early as the middle of the second century, the Christian religion had spread into northern Arabia, Mesopotamia, Media, Persia, Parthia, and Bactria,—in some of which places it had been planted in the previous century; and it soon after (180) penetrated even as far as India. Alexandria, in Egypt, it had previously reached; and thence it had been propagated into neighboring regions, having progressed as far as the Thebaid in Upper Egypt, Proconsular, or northern, Africa was christianized early in this period by missionaries from Rome; and of the churches there established, that in Alexandria and that in Carthage were soon numbered among the most flourishing and distinguished in Christendom.

In the West, churches were founded in Lyons and Vienne, in Gaul, now France, by missionaries from Asia Minor,—among whom was Irenæus,—in the middle of the second century; and from these a knowledge of the Gospel was spread not only into other parts of Gaul, but also into Germany, and perhaps also into Britain; though it is not improbable that Britain itself, as well as Gaul, received Christianity not mediately but directly from Asia Minor. Irenæus testifies to the existence in his time of churches in Spain,—where, perhaps, the Gospel may have been first preached by

Paul,—and also in Germany; and he speaks of "***many nations*** of barbarians who, without paper and ink, have, through the Holy Spirit, the words of salvation written in their hearts". Tertullian goes still further, and speaks, somewhat rhetorically, of all the Spanish territories, the various Gallic nations, the Germans, and of "the regions of the Britains, inaccessible to the Romans but subject to Christ", as places and people to which the Gospel had come, and among which the name of Christ was dominant.

It is certain that before the close of the second century, Christianity had been planted in Britain. The ecclesiastical historian Eusebius (†340) carries the origin of the British churches back into the first century, and says that the Gospel was preached to the Britons by an Apostle. His testimony on this point is not quite satisfactory; for his belief was perhaps based upon a probably erroneous interpretation of that passage in the Epistle of Clement of Rome where he testifies that Paul traveled "to the boundary of the West". According to Bede (†735), Lucius, a British (perhaps a Welsh) prince, sent, in the latter part of the second century (about 176), to Eleutheros, bishop of Rome, and obtained from him missionaries for evangelizing Britain. But this mode of accounting for the universally admitted existence of churches in Britain at this period, is scarcely allowable; for the whole narrative bears too evident marks of having been invented by the Romish Anglo-Saxon clergy of later days, from a desire to establish in Britain the spiritual supremacy of Rome. The tradition is received with suspicion by Mosheim; who feels confident, that, if Lucius sent anywhere for Christian teachers, he sent to Gaul; and agrees with the most reliable British writers in supposing that prince to have been at most only the restorer and second father of the British churches, and not their original founder. The account given by Bede is discredited also by Neander, and by other historians; who conclude, with good reason, from several circumstances,—but particularly from the character of the church worship and festivals of the ancient British congregations, which, differing in not a few points from those of the Church of Rome and the communities formed under its influence, corresponded much more nearly with the ritual of the churches of the East,—that the original churches of Britain were founded,—if not by one of the Apostles or by Christian teachers of the Apostolic Age,—by missionaries coming from Gaul directly, or from the more distant Asia Minor.

By whomsoever planted, Christianity took ready root in Britain; and a number of churches, apostolic in their principles and usages, was established in the island; and, it is said, "a number of royal blood, and many of inferior birth, were called to be saints". Separated from the rest of Europe by their insular position, and, especially during the latter part of this period, subjects of the Roman Emperor rather in name than in reality, the Britons were but little thought of at this time; and are but seldom mentioned in the written records of the closing years of this age. Yet churches of the Gospel pattern flourished among them; and they continued to prosper until, in the next period, the British nation lost its independence at the hands of the pagan Anglo-Saxons.

§2. SPECULATIVE DOCTRINES IN THE APOSTOLIC CHURCH, AND AMONG THE CHRISTIAN FATHERS.

Christ not the Author of Doctrines in a Scientific Form—The Doctrines of the Church as Developed by the Apostles—John and Paul the Chief Apostolic Doctrinal Writers—Freedom of Speculative Opinion in the Apostolic Age—Difference between the Jewish and the Gentile Christians respecting the Mosaic Law—Two-fold Tendency of Doctrinal Error; to Judaism, and to Ethnicism—Doctrinal Speculation in the Early Church—Rise of "Gnosis", or "*Science, falsely so Called*"?Phase of Religious Speculation at the End of the Apostolic Age—Relapse into Gnosticism—Platonism of the Christian Fathers—The "Person of Christ", and the "Origin of Evil"—Speculation discountenanced in the West—The First Schisms in the Church.

JESUS, the Author and Finisher of the Christian's Faith, revealed the life-giving truths which he imparted to mankind in a style that was simple and adapted to the comprehension of the common mind. He spoke for the most part in figures and in parables. The revelation of himself and of his divine mission to save humanity, was the end and aim of his teachings. In thus giving instruction, he taught doctrines indeed, living, soul-penetrating doctrines; but he did not attempt to inculcate them with scientific exactness, after the manner of most earthly instructors. The promulgation of Christian truth in a scientific doctrinal form, he left to the Apostles, his successors in the Church.

The doctrine of the Apostles is found in certain books of the New Testament. Of the original "Twelve", however, we have doctrinal writings from only two, *Pe-*

ter and John; for it is disputed whether the James and Jude from whom we have Epistles, were the Apostles of that name, or those known as brothers of the Lord. To Peter and John must be added *Paul,* specially called, after our Lord's resurrection, "to be an-Apostle". The writings of these three alone are, strictly speaking, Apostolic,—the other doctrinal books of the New Testament not being immediately, but mediately, Apostolic; though they come to us under full Apostolic sanction and authority.

The writings of Peter are rather practical than doctrinal; and that which is purely doctrinal in them is not stated with the scientific fullness and order which characterize the dogmatic teachings of John and Paul. These two Apostles, John and Paul,—the one eminently contemplative, the other dialectical and practical,— are they who have laid the basis of Christian doctrinal scientific speculation for all time.—The appearance of God in the flesh; the communion of man with God through Christ; the life that comes from and centres in God, and the victory over the world and over sin through this life, which is a life of love; this, it has been well said, is the ground-tone of the Johannean intuition of Christianity. Paul has different mental characteristics; and though he teaches the same Gospel as John, he presents it from the stand-point of his own peculiar Christian consciousness. John dwells rather upon the phase of the doctrines of Christianity which relates to *God* and to *Christ;* Paul, upon that which relates to *man* and to *the plan of salvation.* Still, however, John's writings possess the highest importance *anthropologically,* and Paul's *theologically* and christologically; *but the central-point of John's dogmatic theology is* the Word (Logos) become flesh in Christ; *of Paul's, the doctrine of* justification by faith.

Much freedom of speculative opinion was allowed in the Apostolic Age of the Church. It was only when a doctrine was opposed to the religious and moral interests of Christianity, that it was resisted, even by the Apostles themselves, as an evil which demanded immediate and absolute correction.—Even a positive error, if not practically scandalous, and if it did not trench upon the fundamental principles of Christianity, was tolerated, according to Apostolic precept and example; provided that it did not claim for itself exclusive adoption, and was not urged in such a way as was calculated to produce schism in the church. A positive error of an important moral and religious bearing, however, was not allowed to be entertained without

Apostolic reproof and opposition; and even those errors which sprang from unauthorized inferences from doctrines which are true, if they led to a moral abuse of the doctrine, were sharply condemned. But mere speculative opinion on points not of a distinct moral bearing, was universally tolerated in the Apostolic Age of the Church.

It is supposed by some that the doctrines of Christianity were held in the utmost purity by nearly all believers in the Apostolic Age. This supposition is quite erroneous. The early churches, whether in Palestine or among the Gentiles, were not unfrequently troubled by those who both held error themselves and sought to turn others away from the simple truths of the Gospel. The Apostolic Epistles prove this fact beyond possibility of dispute. Paul frequently alludes to such a state of things; and John gives a picture, in the Apocalypse, of the state of the principal churches in Asia Minor, which can be looked upon only in one light, as proof positive and convincing.

One who has read the Acts of the Apostles attentively; must have noticed that a difference of opinion, and consequently of practice, existed from the beginning, between the Jewish and the Gentile Christians, as to the extent of the application of the Mosaic Law to the Gentile Churches—a difference which was pressed upon so hard by Jewish teachers at Antioch, that it was found advisable to refer the matter to the decision of a council composed of the Apostles and Elders of the church in Jerusalem. The Council decided that the Gentiles were released from all obligation to perform the requirements of the Jewish ceremonial Law, except those known as the "seven precepts of Noah". Difference of opinion, however, upon this same point, between the Jewish and the Gentile Christians, continued still to exist, notwithstanding the decision of the Apostolic Council. Among the Jewish Christians, a party yet remained who asserted that the Mosaic Law was binding on the Gentiles; while among the Gentile Christians, the teachings of Paul soon led to the legitimate inference that the Gentile believers were bound in no respect by the Mosaic ceremonial regulations. Paul himself combats rigorously, especially in his Epistle to the Galatians, the error of those Judaizing instructors, who wished to impose the burden of the Mosaic law upon those who believed among the Gentiles.

The first danger, then, in a doctrinal point of view, to which Christianity was exposed, was a relapse into ceremonial Judaism. The stricter among the Jewish

Christians continued to insist that Gentile believers should conform to the Law of Moses; and this determination of theirs, which grew only stronger by the lapse of: time, though it produced no open schism in the Church, resulted, after the destruction of Jerusalem, in the formation of a distinct Jewish party. This party came in time to be distinguished by the appellation ***Ebionites,***—a sect which held the Mosaic Law to be binding in all cases, and that Jesus was the son, not of God, but of Joseph and Mary.

On the Gentile side, the doctrines of Christianity were exposed to corrupting influences of another kind,—to a mingling with the theosophic speculations and mythological tendencies of Heathenism. This danger exhibited itself quite early in the Church as established among the Gentiles; very soon, in fact, after philosophy began to have a part in the treatment of the doctrines of Christianity. Apollos, a cultivated Jew of Alexandria, was the first to regard and speak of the doctrines of Christianity from a speculative point of view; and he gained thereby distinguished reputation, especially among the Christians of Corinth. Such a philosophical treatment of Christianity by Apollos and others,—which was correct enough, and altogether allowable, so long as it was merely speculative,?was received favorably in many of the Gentile Churches; but it soon overstepped the bounds of moderation, and became the means of introducing into the Churches, first of all in Asia Minor, the superstitious heathen philosophy of the times. Thus was laid the basis of that corruption of Christian doctrine which has been well denominated "Ethnicism". This philosophy, this "science (***gnosis***) falsely so called",—especially when it mingled, as it often did, with a Jewish-heathen asceticism,—not only tended to subvert the simplicity of the Gospel, but endangered morality itself, "by recommending chimerical mysterious doctrines, and an arbitrary asceticism, as the true mode of purifying the soul". These corruptions met, in their incipient stage, with rigorous resistance from the Apostle Paul[11].

Paul was not opposed to philosophy as such, as is proved by his fraternal conduct towards Apollos; but he did reject philosophy "falsely so called",—that heathen and false ***Gnosis*** ("science") which, as he had predicted respecting its essence, did, at length, even before John's death, come into conflict with the fundamental

---

11   See Col. 2: 8, 16, ss.; 1 Tim. 1: 4—7, 4: 3, 7, 6: 20; 2 Tim. 2: 18 (coll. 1 Thess. 4, 13, ss.; 1 Cor. 15: 12, 35, ss.); 2 Tim. 3:1, RS.

principles of Christianity.

Religious speculation assumed a more scientific form in the latter part of the Apostolic Age. It now engaged itself chiefly with attempts to understand and to explain scientifically, "the wonderful person of Christ". In this it only followed along the path which had been trodden by the Apostle John in his Gospel. These speculations, had they confined themselves within the limits of human wisdom, would not have been injurious perhaps in their influence upon the doctrines of the Church. They soon, however, overleaped the bounds of propriety. So long as they did not trench upon the two-fold nature of Christ, they were allowed; but when they impaired the union of the divine and the human in our Lord,—as did the doctrine of the Docetœ, which represented his humanity as a mere appearance (a *phantasm*), and not a reality (cp. 1 Jno. 4: 2, 2 Jno. 7),—they were rejected and condemned.

In Syria and Egypt, and in the East generally,—especially in those cities in which the Jewish-Alexandrian philosophy prevailed,—speculations on the higher nature of Christ, and respecting the essence of Christianity, became involved with the more general questions concerning the creation of the world and the origin of evil. Hence arose the Christian Gnostic systems of the East, which, were engrafted by certain speculative minds, early in this period, upon the teachings of Christianity,—those mixed systems of Christianity, Jewish Theology, and Eastern Theosophy and Mythology, which were received with no little favor by not a few of those who were given to speculation in the first centuries of the Christian Church. In the time of the last of the Christian Fathers above spoken of, *Gnosticism* had quite generally developed itself into undoubted heresy,—the denial of some of the most essential doctrines of Apostolic Christianity.

Gnosticism, however, was not the only form of religious speculation current in this period. *Platonism,*—which of all the heathen philosophical systems stands nearest to Christianity,—being introduced by Platonic Philosophers, who were now converted to the truth, was engrafted in this age upon the teachings of the New Testament. Such a speculative treatment of Christianity, as it now received from believers who had been instructed in the Platonic philosophy, was rendered necessary by the course taken by the Gnostics; whose errors it was highly important to combat. It was, perhaps, advisable and proper, moreover, in order to bring the Christian religion, and its doctrines in contact with the philosophically cultivated heathen minds of the time. If error sprung from the commingling of philosophy with Christianity, it arose from the imperfection of human reason, and not from any inherent fault of philosophy; for Christianity and the true and highest philosophy are one and the same.

Our Christian philosophers,—and nearly all the Fathers were philosophers, in a greater or less degree,—occupied themselves in their speculations chiefly and with the same questions which engaged the attention of the Gnostics,—the Divine nature of Jesus; and the origin of evil, and its overthrow by Christ. The Doctrine of the *Logos* ("Word"), his relation to God and to man, was especially discussed. It was fully developed from the Old Testament, viewed from the stand-point of the Platonic philosophy, by a mystic and unnatural interpretation which often produced more error than it elicited truth.

These speculations were carried on freely in the bosom of the Church; for now, as in the times of the Apostles, "ecclesiastical orthodoxy could still endure", as Gieseler correctly remarks, "diversities in doctrine and customs, which did not injure the religious basis of Christianity". This theological speculation, however, was confined almost wholly, for the first three centuries, to the East; the churches of the West being generally averse to it, both from their dislike of philosophy, and from their ignorance of the original languages of the Scriptures, which prevented them from attempting for themselves an independent development of Theology. The western churches, therefore, were not as yet agitated by theological controversy; and they knew but little of the discussions which were going on in the East.

Even in the East, the discussions which were there carried on, did not for some time, result in any open schism in the Church. Though heretical sentiments, and heretical parties, were condemned, those who held them did not necessarily form a schismatical party out of the communion of the Church Catholic. The first ecclesiastical schism, properly so called, was that of Felicissimus in Carthage (251), which, however, did not long continue. It was contemporary in origin with the noted schism of Novatian in Rome; conducted by a party which "was widely extended, and continued for a long time". Both of these schisms were produced, not by discussions upon speculative doctrines, but by controversies respecting matters of church discipline. The same is true of the schism of Meletius (306), and of that of Donatus (313),—which latter, however, arose in Carthage a few years before its leadership was assumed by Donatus.

§3. CONSTITUTION AND GOVERNMENT OF THE CHURCH.

Change in the Relations of Presbyters—The Presiding Presbyter, Bishop, or Pastor—Comparison of the Christian Church Officers with the Jewish Priesthood—A more Definite Distinction between the Clergy and the Laity—The Clergy a Sacred and Holy Class—The Churches, at first, still Independent—Deference to Apostolic Churches—Church Officers still Elected by the Church—New Officers—Powers of the Bishop—The Beginning of the Diocesan Church Constitution—Two Productive Causes; the Influence of the City, particularly Apostolic, Churches, and the Holding of Synods—The First Synods, or Associations—Synods had originally no Jurisdiction over the Churches, being merely Conventional, or Associational, Assemblies—Encroachment upon the Powers of the Churches—Final Formation of the Diocesan, or Metropolitan, Constitution,—and this developed at length into the Patriarchal.

It was found, in our consideration of the Church Government of the former period, that a change in the relative powers of certain Officers in the church individual had already taken place some time before the close of the Apostolic Age, even before the death of the "Apostle of the Gentiles"; that one from among the Presbyters had been elevated, for the sake of the better management of each church, under the title of Bishop, or President, above the rest of the College of Presbyters, in those congregations which were governed by a plurality of Presbyters, or Elders. This was especially true of the church in Jerusalem. Its example was imitated by the neighboring churches; and especially by the Christian congregation in Antioch. Ignatius urgently recommends, in his Epistles, the universal adoption of such an episcopate. This, however, was not, by any means, like the ***episcopate*** as known in our day; but rather resembled, and in all important respects was quite identical with, the ***pastorate*** as understood, now-a-days, among all well-ordered congregational churches. These presiding Officers, along with the appellation Bishops, or Presidents, still retained, for a long time, the title Presbyters,—being in reality, at first, little more than the ***presiding Officers*** of the College of Elders.

Though the idea of a universal Christian priesthood was still maintained, and the brotherhood were allowed in urgent cases to perform the offices of baptizing and of administering the Lord's Supper, yet the *Clergy* as a separate order, in contradistinction from the *Laity,* had been, previously to the commencement of this period, and even in the lifetime of the Apostles, everywhere recognized; and their support was provided for as a matter of divine appointment.

The form of government,—call it episcopal, or pastoral,—which we find already fully established in the churches in the very beginning of the second century, assumed, at length,—from peculiar influences then operating in the churches,— particularly towards the close of this period, a decidedly monarchical character. The causes tending to produce this change were several; but the most operative of all, perhaps, was the practice, now grown quite common, of comparing the Mosaic with the Christian institutions, and of considering the former a type of the latter. This practice, which originated early in the history of the Church, and which became quite universal after the final destruction of Jerusalem, led naturally to the supposition of a correspondence of the Officers of the Christian Church with the different classes of the Jewish priesthood. The Bishops, accordingly, were thought to have come in the room of the High Priests; the Presbyters, of the Priests; and the Deacons, of the Levites.

At the close of this period, the lines of demarkation between the Clergy and the Laity had been so distinctly drawn, at least in Asia, Africa, and Southern Europe, that a peculiar mystic influence was ascribed to the *ordinations* which the former performed; and "they now", as Gieseler testifies, "appeared in the character of persons appointed by God himself to be the medium of communication between Him and the Christian world". No change in the ecclesiastical constitution has ever been more fundamental than this; and none has produced more pernicious results in the whole history of the Christian Church. Its direct tendency is, and its influence has always been, to take away the feeling of individual responsibility from the minds of the Laity, and utterly to destroy all personal religion.

During the first part of this period, the churches were still, as in Apostolic times, in general, ***independent of each other;*** though some among them had a higher reputation than the rest on account of their Apostolic origin and training. These were not unfrequently appealed to on controverted points of doctrine or ecclesiastical usage, as being most likely to be informed of the teachings of the Apostles. Each church, however, was still, and continued to be, as a general rule, at least as late as the middle of the second century, entirely independent of the judicial control of another congregation, or association of congregations. As Mosheim describes it, each church was "a kind of small, independent republic, governing itself by its own laws, enacted, or at least sanctioned, by the people."

Every city church was, during this period, presided over by its ***Bishop,*** who had been either directly elected by the brotherhood, or had been appointed with their consent. As a council of advice, and as assistants in his pastoral supervision, he had a college of fellow Presbyters, whose places and duties he determined; and, subordinate to the Presbyters, a body of Deacons, and a sisterhood of Deaconesses, proportionate to the size and importance of the Church. In some congregations, towards the close of the period, other subordinate officers,—sub-deacons, readers, singers, door-keepers, attendants, and exorcists,—had been created for special purposes, or to meet what were considered new necessities.

The extent of the jurisdiction of the Bishop in the first part of this age, is thus described by one who follows the representation given by the historian Mosheim: "It consisted in the administration of the sacraments and discipline of the church; the superintendency of religious ceremonies, which imperceptibly increased in number and variety; the consecration of ecclesiastical ministers, to whom the bishop assigned their respective functions; the management of the public fund; and the determination of all such differences as the faithful were unwilling to expose before the tribunal of an idolatrous judge. These powers, during a short period, were exercised according to the advice of the presbyterial college, and with the consent and approbation of the assembly of Christians."

A change from the congregational into the diocesan, or metropolitan, church organization, was induced, at length, by the operation in particular of two all-powerful causes. The first of these was the gradual extension of the power of the city bishops over the clergy of the neighboring country churches. As the number of Christians in the country adjacent to the cities increased, separate congregations were constituted in suitable places; and each of these either attached itself to the nearest city church, and received from its bishop a presbyter, sometimes a deacon, for its president; or else it chose its own bishop, who, however, from the force of circumstances, soon became dependent to a certain extent on the president of the church in the city. In this way, the bishops of the city churches kept extending their jurisdiction beyond the bounds of a single church and the congregations assembling in one city; until, at length, they were converted, by this process and that which is about to be mentioned, into metropolitan, or diocesan, bishops, corresponding in all important particulars to the diocesan bishops of the present day. Thus was laid the first stone of the foundation of episcopal domination in nearly every land in which Christianity has yet been propagated.

About the middle of the second century, there arose a new ecclesiastical institution, which, though originally useful and healthful in its influence, totally changed, within two hundred years, the ecclesiastical constitution of the whole Church. This was the ***Provincial Synod.*** Developed itself, no doubt, from the extension of the episcopal jurisdiction beyond the bounds of a single city,—that is, from the ***parochial*** organization,—this institution was the second chief cause which operated in producing the change which now took place from the congregational to the diocesan organization of the Church. Previous to this time, each Christian society, as we have seen, "formed within itself", to use the words of Gibbon, "a separate and independent republic: and although the most distant of these little, states maintained a mutual as well as friendly intercourse of letters and deputations, the Christian world was not yet connected by any supreme authority or legislative assembly."— But now a change occurred.

The first Synods of which we have any account were held (in 160-170) in Greece, the seat of the Amphictyonic Councils, to deliberate respecting the Montanists, and respecting the time of celebrating Easter. Tertullian, in his book "***On Fasts***" (***De Jejuniis***), written about the year 200, thus describes them (c. 13): "Throughout Greece, in fixed places, are held these Councils, composed of all the churches; and, by means of them, both those matters which are of unusual importance are considered in common, and the representation of the whole Christian name is solemnized with great veneration."

From this time forth similar Synods assembled stately in Greece, and, soon after, in Asia Minor and North Africa, once or twice a year; and, before the third century had drawn to a close, these provincial Councils were, it is probable, regularly held throughout the Christian world.

The Synods were composed of the Bishops and Presbyters of a province; acting, at first, as representatives of their respective congregations, and assembled to consult and deliberate on matters of common interest to the churches in each province, but not to legislate respecting, nor in any way to interfere with, the private affairs of individual congregations. They possessed, and claimed, at first, no jurisdiction; but "were mere conventions of delegates, met to consider and agree upon matters of common concernment". They were, in a word,—if we except the fact that only bishops and presbyters were representatives of the churches,—precisely such organizations as the Baptist Conventions, or Associations, of the present day; and the objects of their meeting were, in all essential particulars, precisely the same. Had they continued true to their original intent, their influence in and upon the Church could not have been other than salutary.

These Synods, however, did not for any long time retain their original character. As the Councils were convened, for the most part, in the principal city of each province, under the presidency of the bishop of that city,—upon whom the neighboring country bishops (or presbyters) were already in some measure dependent,—the bishops of the churches in these principal cities gradually obtained, partly by their own efforts, and partly by the voluntary consent, and, perhaps, express appointment, of the other representatives, a kind of superintendence over the rest of the bishops in their provinces.—The delegates, moreover, denied, after a time, that they were only the representatives of the churches, and, as such, acting under human authority; and claimed the right, as representatives of Christ, to enact and enforce laws, to hear and decide controversies, and to bind and control the churches by their canons and regulations.—Thus were subverted at one and the same time, by means of the Synods, the original perfect equality of the bishops, and the independence of the churches.

The character of these Provincial Synods, after they had departed from their original intention, is thus described by the historian Gibbon,—truthfully, upon the whole, but with his usual spirit, when speaking of the institutions of Christianity: "Their deliberations were assisted by the advice of a few distinguished presbyters, and moderated by the presence of a listening multitude. Their decrees, which were styled Canons, regulated every important controversy of faith and discipline; and it was natural to believe that a liberal effusion of the Holy Spirit would be poured out on the united assembly of the delegates of the Christian people.—The institution of synods was so well suited to private ambition and to public interest, that in the space of a few years it was received throughout the whole empire.—A regular correspondence was established between the provincial councils, which mutually communicated and approved their respective proceedings; and the catholic church soon assumed the form, and acquired the strength, of a great federative republic."

By the natural operation of the Synods there was introduced, as has been mentioned, a prëeminence of rank among the Bishops themselves; and thence a superiority of jurisdiction. The chief bishop in each province became, in time, an archbishop, or **Metropolitan** and, at length, in the reign of Constantine (†337),—when Provincial Synods were held throughout the Roman world, and when the Church, save here and there a distant member, had assumed the form of a vast monarchy composed of a multitude of smaller ones,—there were introduced the **Patriarchs,** formed of the metropolitans of Rome, Antioch, Alexandria, and Constantinople; and from these was developed, in later days, the prince of Patriarchs, the **Pope of Rome.** He, however, became the head and ruler of Papal Christianity only; not of the true Church, the bride and body of Christ.

§4. CHURCH USAGES AND ORDINANCES NOT BAPTISMAL.

Public Worship, though at first still Simple, encumbered, at length, with Rites and Ceremonies—The First Christian Houses of Worship—Time of Holding Meetings—Other Sacred Seasons besides the Lord's Day—Justin Martyr's Account of the Mode of Church Worship, and the Usages therewith Connected—The Ordinance of the Lord's Supper?Justin's Account of its Administration—The Terms of Church Communion—Only the Baptized admitted to the Ordinance—Testimony of Bunsen's "Hippolytus"—Reading of the New Testament Scriptures in the Church Assemblies—Gradual Formation of the New Testament Canon—The "Gospel" and the "Apostolic Discourses"—Brief Statement of the Dates of the New Testament Canonical Books—Authors of the Books of the New Testament Canon—Spurious Writings in the Early Churches—The Universal "Rule of Faith"—"Apostolic Tradition"—Times of Fasting and Prayer—Restoration of Excluded Church Members—The "Confessors".

Public worship was still quite simple during the first part of this period; but, towards its close, a number of additions was made to the rites and ceremonies of the Church, which resulted, after a time, in the total corruption of some of them throughout almost all the Christian world. Various rites and ceremonies were then added to the originally simple worship of the churches, in order to give it external pomp and splendor; and, in this way, to render Christianity more attractive to the multitude. New rites were connected with the two ordinances of the Church; and the ordinances themselves began to be regarded, and to be called, the Christian Mysteries, at which no person doing penance, nor any one not baptized, was allowed to be present,—a practice derived, there is no doubt, from the heathen "Mysteries".

Near the end of the second century we find mention made of buildings here and there devoted exclusively to the worship of God. Up to this time the brethren had possessed no temples, or houses dedicated solely to the service of God; but had assembled, for the most part, in rooms of private houses appointed for the purpose, and, in times of persecution, in caves and in other solitary places. The erection of houses consecrated wholly to God having been once commenced, elegant and imposing edifices soon began to be constructed.

The religious meetings of the churches were held, as in the previous century, on the Lord's Day, and sometimes also on the seventh day of the week, or Saturday. Not unfrequently the Christian congregation met at night; sometimes, just before the dawn of day. Pliny the younger, governor of Bithynia, in Asia Minor, testifies, in his noted letter written to the Emperor Trajan about 110 A. D., that the Christians of his province,—who were so numerous even then in Bithynia, that, as he declares, "the contagion of their superstition had spread not only through the cities, but into the villages, and throughout the country",—were accustomed, according to their own accounts, "to assemble, , *on a stated day,* before light, and sing a hymn to Christ as God". This day, no doubt, was Sunday; and it is so styled expressly by Justin Martyr.

Besides Sunday, which was commemorated as a *weekly* festival, the churches in this period, particularly towards its close, generally observed the *yearly* festival of the Passover, or Easter, as a day commemorative of the death of Christ: but one season was celebrated by the churches of the East, and another and different by those of the West. In the East, the day was observed as the anniversary of the Jewish Passover feast, with reference to Christ as the paschal lamb; in the West, as the anniversary, in particular, of his resurrection from the dead.

Justin Martyr,—who was personally acquainted with most of the principal churches of Apostolic foundation, and who had visited, in his travels, many of the most important and most flourishing congregations in nearly every part of the Roman Empire,—gives, in his longer "Apology" (139 A. D.), a very valuable account of the mode of worship practised in the assemblies of the brotherhood in his day. We learn from his description that the churches worshipped God during the first half of the second century, and observed the ordinances of His house, with the same becoming simplicity as in the Apostolic and primitive age of the Church.

In this Apology, Justin thus describes the mode of church worship and the usages connected with it, as customary in the early part of this period: "On the day called Sunday, we all, both those who dwell in the towns and those who live in the villages, assemble together.—The Memoirs of the Apostles [the *Gospels,* it is most probable], and the writings of the Prophets [the prophetical Books of the Old Testament], are read as long as the time will permit. The reader having ended, the President [*Proestos*], makes an application, in an address, and exhorts to an imitation of these excellent examples.—Then, we all rise up together, and pour forth united prayers.—When we have finished the prayers, bread, as I have already said, and wine and water are brought forward; and the President, in like manner, offers prayers and thanksgivings, according to his ability; and the people respond, saying, *Amen.* A distribution and participation of what has been blessed thereupon take place to each one present; and to those who are absent, it is sent by the Deacons.

"Those who are prosperous and willing, give what they choose, each according to his own pleasure. What is collected is deposited with the President; and he carefully relieves the orphans and widows, and those who, from sickness or other causes, are in want; and also those who are in prison, and the strangers resident with us, and, in short, all who have need of help.

"We make Sunday the day of our assembling together in common, because the *first* day (of the week) is that on which God, having changed darkness and chaos, made the world; and because on the same day Jesus Christ, our Saviour, arose from the dead."—Such is the account given by Justin.

The elements of the Lord's Supper, and the materials for the *Agape* (*or, love-feast*),—which, as is known from other testimony, was still held in many places, as had been the case in the Apostolic age, in connection with the Eucharist, though it is not mentioned in the account of Justin, and may, as early as this, have fallen into disuse in the congregations immediately under his eye,—were taken from the voluntary offerings brought by the members of the church. The remainder of these offerings,—which, as early as the time of Justin, were considered oblations sacred to God, and were compared with the Old Testament sacrifices and first-fruits,—served for the maintenance of the clergy and of the poor; for whom additional provision was made, when necessary, by monthly contributions.

In another part of the Apology which has been quoted from, Justin, in detailing the ceremonies practised on the reception of new members into the Christian community, mentions the Lord's Supper as the final rite connected with the ceremony of initiation. He takes occasion, therefore, to describe the mode of its administration.

"Then", he proceeds,—that is, after the prayers offered in behalf of those who have been baptized into the communion of the Church,—"there are placed before the President bread and a cup of water and wine; and he taking them offers praise and glory to the Father of all things, through the name of the Son and of the Holy Spirit; and gives thanks at great length, because we are accounted worthy of these things at His hands. When he has ended the prayers and the thanksgiving, all the people present respond, *Amen.* . . . . . After the President has given thanks, and all the people have uttered the response, those whom we call Deacons distribute to each one of those present, that each may partake of the bread, and wine, and water, which have been blessed; and they carry (a portion) to those not present. This food is called by us the *Eucharist* [because it had been *blessed*]; which it is unlawful for any one to partake of, unless he believes the things taught by us to be true [that is, is a professed believer in Christ], and has been cleansed with the washing for the remission of sins in regeneration [that is, has been baptized], and lives according to what Christ has taught."

The terms of Church Communion are here expressly laid down by Justin. No one could partake of the Lord's Supper, unless he was a believer in Christ, had been baptized, and led a moral life in accordance with the precepts of the Saviour. And this is precisely the doctrine of the Baptists of the present day; and it has been the doctrine of all consistent Baptists in every period of Christianity.

Chevalier Bunsen, in the third volume of his late work, (p. 184) on "Hippolytus and his Age",—in which he treats of the Education, Baptism, and Worship of the Church during the latter part of the second and first half of the third century; and in which he proves incontestably, from the written documents of this period, that, as far as regards the Act of Baptism, and as regards its subjects, the usages of the Church were still essentially the same at this time as in the latter half of the first century, and, consequently, the same as those of the Baptists of the present time,—thus testifies, on the ground of ancient usage and of logical consistency, to the propriety of restricting, as did the ancient Christians, church communion to baptized believers. "Nothing", he says, "can be more natural; for the celebration of the Lord's Supper was the solemn act of believers; and implied reception into the Christian community, of which it was intended to be the sacred symbol. No one can take part in the solemn ceremony of a close society, except one who has been received into it. To have allowed it, would have been a contradiction in terms."

This work of Bunsen's is based on a recently discovered (1842) Treatise of Hippolytus,—a pupil of Irenæus,—on "Heresies", composed about 225 A. D.; and upon genuine ancient Canons, Constitutions, and church Liturgies, composed before the time of Hippolytus. Making use of these sources of information, Mr. Bunsen,—who is a scholar of eminence, and has been, for many years, the Prussian Ambassador at the British Court,—has drawn up, and presented to the world,—in three volumes in English, and one in German,—an account of the usages and doctrines of the Church in the beginning of the third century after Christ.

The conclusions at which he arrives respecting Baptism and the Lord's Supper, as practised at this time in the Church, and respecting the relation between these ordinances, as then existing, correspond almost wholly with the views held by the Baptists Of course, he makes ***immersion alone*** baptism; and though himself a Pædo-baptist and an advocate of Pædo-baptism, he declares that the ordinance was ***never*** administered to infants, during the century succeeding the age of the Apostles. He traces the origin of infant baptism,—how justly we shall see hereafter,—to the baptism of children (not ***infants***) as practised at an early period, certainly as early as the time of Tertullian (†220), in the church of Alexandria, in Egypt.

The work of Hippolytus was first published in 1851; at which time it was thought to be the long-lost treatise of Origen (†254) on the "Heresies". It now turns out to have been written by Hippolytus, bishop of Portus, in Italy

Besides the Old Testament,—particularly the Prophetic Books,—there were read quite generally in the churches, early in this period, the Gospels, and the genuine Apostolic writings; and, in some congregations, other writings besides, not Apostolic. As the churches had now come into close connection, and as it became necessary, on the death of the Apostles, to have some authoritative standard of faith and practice, in order to prevent heresy and schism, the churches early communicated to each other the genuine writings of the Apostles. Thus there soon began to be formed, in two parts (the Gospels, and the Apostolic Epistles), the canon of the New Testament Scriptures. The Old Testament Canon had long before been completed.—By the middle of the second century, "most of the books composing the New Testament", Mosheim remarks, "were in every Christian church throughout the known world; and they were read, and were regarded as the divine rule of faith and practice." These books, however, did not exist quite as early as this in a collected form.

No collection of the New Testament writings seems to have been made by any of the Apostles themselves; not even by John, as an unreliable ecclesiastical tradition, of late origin, would have us believe. The formation of the New Testament Canon, as we now possess it, was a gradual process. Ignatius speaks of the "Gospel" and the "Epistles"; and Irenæus makes mention of the same. Clement of Alexandria frequently refers to the? "Gospels" and the "Apostolic Discourses"; and Tertullian speaks as if the Canon were complete in his time. We are justified, therefore, in inferring that the New Testament Scriptures existed in a collected form, and were generally known and possessed in this collected form in the principal churches, at least as early as the middle of the third century.

The books admitted into the Canon were the same as those now generally received; for the writings belonging to it, as enumerated by Origen and by Eusebius, are, with one or two apparent exceptions[12], the same as those now contained in the New Testament. Of *ten* ancient catalogues of the New Testament Scriptures still extant, *six* agree precisely with, our present Canon: of the rest, *three* omit only the

---

12   Eusebius says of the Epistles of James and Jude, the 2d Epistle of Peter, the 2d and 3rd Epistles of John, and the Apocalypse, that they were doubted by some, but *received by the majority,*

Apocalypse (Revelation), and the *fourth* omits the Apocalypse and the Epistle to the Hebrews.

The writings contained in the New Testament are 1.) the *four* Gospels; 2.) the Acts; 3.) the *fourteen* Pauline Epistles; 4.) the *seven* Catholic Epistles (called "Catholic", most probably, from the encyclical character of the five longest); and 5.) the Apocalypse.

1.—Of these writings, the Pauline Epistles are the New Testament books whose composition was first commenced; and they were the earliest in use in the churches. The oldest among them, the 1st Epistle to the Thessalonians, was composed in 52 or 53 A. D., some twenty years after the crucifixion of our Lord. The latest of these writings is the 2d Epistle to Timothy, composed, most probably, during a second imprisonment of Paul in Rome.

2.—Of the Gospels, Matthew's was, doubtless, the earliest; it having been written, most probably, a few years before the destruction of Jerusalem. Irenæus dates its composition at the time Peter and Paul were in Rome (between 64 and 67 A. D). The Gospel of John was the last composed; having been written, most likely, in Ephesus (some say, Patmos), somewhere between the year 70 and the latter part of the first century.? "Acts" was written, most likely, about 64, A. D.

3.—Of the Catholic Epistles, that of James (probably, James, "the brother of the Lord"), and the two of Peter, were the first written: the former, not long before James, martyrdom (69 A. D.); the latter, between 64 and 67 A. D. John's three Epistles were, it is well established, composed after his Gospel. The Epistle of Jude (whether of Jude, the Apostle, or of Jude, the Lord's brother, is doubtful,—if indeed the two were different persons) was written, most likely, late in the century, after the destruction of Jerusalem (perhaps, as late as 90 A. D.).

4.—The Apocalypse was composed, the weight of evidence goes to show, somewhere between 67 and 69 A. D., perhaps on the isle of Patmos.

The New Testament Canon included only such books as, according to the judgment of the Apostolic churches, had proceeded either from an Apostle, or from one writing under apostolic direction, or with heavenly wisdom,—only such books, in fine, as were accounted by them to be divinely inspired. Not a few writings (Gospels, as well as Epistles) which were held in honor, and statedly read, at this period, in some churches, were, in consequence of not meeting the necessary requirement, excluded from the canon of inspiration.

The number of **spurious** Gospels, Epistles, and Apocalypses, in existence during this period, was greater than the number of genuine canonical New Testament Scriptures. Some of them were even read in the churches; but not so generally as the true Apostolic writings and certain genuine, but uninspired, writings of the Apostolic Fathers. As the settlement of the Canon took place, however, these spurious productions declined in authority, and fell gradually into disuse. Many of these forgeries are still in existence; but the majority are lost. Some of those which are extant, are not without historical importance to the New Testament interpreter, and, especially, to the ecclesiastical historiographer.

By means of this New Testament collection, supplemented by Apostolic tradition, the "Rule of Faith" (**Regula Fidei**) of the Church Catholic was sought to be defined and established, in opposition to all heresy and error; but especially in opposition to "the bold speculation of the Gnostics, which sought to lay an entirely foreign basis under Christianity". This "Rule of Faith" was, as Tertullian describes it, "all that doctrine which the churches have received from the Apostles, the Apostles from Christ, Christ from God",—"that complex notion of doctrine", as Gieseler says, "which could be shown, as well in the consciousness of all Christian communities, as also in the Apostolic writings, to be an essential basis of Christianity, and which must remain untouched by, and be necessarily laid at the foundation of, every speculation".

Apostolic Tradition, therefore, as preserved by the churches of Apostolic foundation, was highly esteemed as a source of Christian truth; but it was not yet, as in later times, deemed of equal importance and authority with the written records which had been left behind by the Apostles. It was often appealed to by the Christian Fathers in their controversies with those whom they considered heretics; and was thought by them, in cases where the Apostolic writings were not sufficiently plain, to be the true test and criterion of Apostolic doctrine and practice. The only Apostolic Tradition, however, which they deemed truly genuine and worthy of universal reception, was that which had been preserved in all the Apostolic churches in every part of the world,—such as was common to all Christian, but especially Apostolic, communities.

Irenæus speaks several times in favor of Apostolic Tradition; evidently regarding it as a kind of supplement to the New Testament Scriptures. He recommends an appeal, in doubtful, or disputed, cases, to the consciousness of the most ancient churches of apostolic foundation; and asks, whether, had the Apostles left no writings, it would not have been incumbent on Christians "to follow the order of the traditions which they delivered to those unto whom they committed the churches".—Clement of Alexandria thinks that it would be highly improper for any one "to go beyond the Rule of Faith handed down traditionally by the Church"; and that every one ought to receive the doctrines and ordinances as held by those "who are already in possession of the truth".—Origen says, "Let that ecclesiastical doctrine be preserved which has been delivered, through the order of succession, by the Apostles, and remains in the churches even to the present time: that alone is to be believed truth, which disagrees in no respect from ecclesiastical and apostolic tradition."

Set times of fasting and prayer,—which were held by preference on Wednesdays and Fridays,—were now more generally observed; but all was left, in these respects, to the free choice of the individual, nothing being imposed by the authority of the Christian community.—The passion-time of Jesus was quite generally observed as a season of fasting. ?Celibacy began now to be overvalued; and a certain kind of asceticism was practised by some Christians, "but all forced and artificial asceticism was disapproved".

Public sinners were excluded from the Church and its privileges; and restoration could be secured only by public repentance. Sometimes the term of repentance was much protracted; and, in the churches of Africa, where the more rigorous principles of Montanism prevailed, those who had been guilty of incontinence, murder, or idolatry, were sometimes sentenced to perpetual exclusion.

Those who suffered martyrdom were highly honored; yearly festivals being in some places held in remembrance of their death. The Confessors, or those who stood firm in their Christian belief and integrity amid persecution, had many privileges conferred on them; and were held, as long as they lived, in high estimation by the churches.—Here were germs productive of many a future evil.

§5. BAPTISM AND ITS ATTENDANT USAGES.

Baptism still Immersion; with Occasional Instances of Affusion at the very

End of the Period—Justin Martyr's Description of the Administration of the Rite—Prerequisites to the Reception of the Ordinance—Previous Confession of Faith—Stated Times of Administering Baptism to Candidates—The Administrators—New Rites and Usages connected with the Performance of the Ceremony—Notice of them by Tertullian—Baptism administered by "Trine Immersion"—Significance of "Cheirothesia", or Laying on of Hands, as connected with the Ordinance.

Baptism, the initiatory ordinance of the Church, continued, during this whole period, uncorrupted in its outward form; for it was still, if we except occasional instances of *affusion* (*pouring*),—which, however, was not considered baptism, but only a substitute for that rite,—administered to sick persons supposed to be at the point of death, a total immersion of the candidate in water. The subjects to whom the ordinance was administered, were, also, only such as exercised a personal faith in Christ; until towards the close of the period, when we find the ceremony,—at least in those churches of Africa which were under the influence either of Alexandria or of Carthage,—performed upon children at an age when they were yet incapable of intelligent belief.

Justin Martyr, in the Apology already quoted from, describes the regular and usual manner in which the rite of Baptism was administered to candidates, and the mode of their subsequent reception into a congregation of believers, as practised in the middle of the second century. "As many as are persuaded and believe," he says, "that the things taught and related by us are true, and profess to be able thus to live, are taught to pray and ask of God, with fasting, the of former sins; we praying and fasting together with them. Afterwards, they are conducted by us (to a place) where there is water; and are regenerated [baptized] in the same manner of regeneration as ourselves were; for they then perform the ablution in water, in the name of the Lord God and Father of all, and of our Saviour Jesus Christ, and of the Holy Ghost. . . . . And this washing is called *illumination;* because they who have learned these things [namely, the import and reasons of baptism], are illuminated in mind. . . . . And after thus washing the convinced and consenting person, we conduct him to where the brethren, as we call them, are assembled; and there offer our united supplications, with earnestness, both for ourselves and for the enlightened person, and for all others everywhere; that we may conduct ourselves as becomes those who have received the truth, and by our deeds prove ourselves good citizens, and observers of what is commanded us; so that we may saved with an eternal salvation. And, on ending our prayers, we salute each other with a kiss."—After this followed the administration of the Lord's Supper as already described.

This description of Justin's shows that the ceremony of Baptism was, in the ordinary cases of its administration, in places where Christian congregations had been already formally organized, preceded by instruction, and by fasting and prayer, on the part of the candidate.—The baptismal Confession of faith, which seems, even in the days of the Apostles, to have been required from the candidate at the water's edge, just previous to his immersion, had now become amplified; the recipient of the ordinance, as Tertullian says, "responding somewhat more at length than the Lord has prescribed in the Gospel". This Confession, originally quite simple, and expressive merely of faith in Christ Jesus as the Messiah, was now enlarged, as the wants of the time seemed to require, and included, in a brief form,—in opposition to Jews, heathen, and heretics,?the essentials of Christianity in which all the apostolic churches were agreed. The Confession, which was called *Symbolum,* was in fact a *Creed,* shorter or longer as occasion demanded; and was made by the candidate in response to separate interrogatories put to him by the baptismal administrator.

Baptism began now to be administered, where regular congregations were already established, at stated periods; in some churches, twice a year, at Easter and at Whitsuntide (at the time of the Passover, and that of Pentecost). It was now, for the most part, particularly towards the close of the period, administered only to *catechumens,* or those who had passed through a long preparatory process of instruction in the truths of Christianity.—When, end of this period, the belief began to be entertained, that Baptism was of itself "a full and absolute expiation of sin", and that the soul of him who received the rite "was instantly restored to its original purity and entitled to the promise of eternal salvation", some catechumens preferred to delay the reception of the ordinance; judging it "imprudent to precipitate a salutary rite, which could not be repeated; to throw away an inestimable privilege, which could never be recovered". Thus, no doubt, originated *clinic affusion,* —performed upon persons lying at the point of death, who had put off the reception of the ordinance until the closing period of their lives, on account of its supposed efficacy in cleansing away all the stains of previous guilt, whether inherited or personal.

The baptismal ceremony was usually performed by the bishop, or by the presbyters or deacons of the Church acting under his authority. In the latter part of this age, when it had become the practice to consider the ordinances of the Church as in some sense *mysteries,* none were allowed even to witness the administration of the rite except those who had themselves been baptized. "The candidates", to use the words of Mosheim, when speaking of the second century, "were immersed wholly in water, with invocation of the sacred Trinity, according to the Saviour's precept; after they had repeated the *Creed* (*Symbolum*), and had renounced all their sins and transgressions, especially the *devil* and his *pomp.* "

By the close of the second century, the ceremony of Baptism was thought to comprise four spiritual elements: instruction, examination, the vow, and the initiation (the immersion); and, in consequence, several new usages,?as trine immersion, anointing (*chrism*), signing of the cross, etc.,—had become connected with the administration of the ordinance; some of which marred its simplicity, though they nullified in no way its essential character and validity. What these usages were, may be gathered from the brief accounts of the administration of Baptism given by Tertullian in his treatise "On the Soldier's Crown" (*De Corona Militis*), and in his work. "On Baptism" (*De Baptismo*): "Being about to approach the water, both there, and also in the Church a short time before, we testify, under the hand of the president, that we renounce the devil, his pomp, and his angels. Then we are immersed three times; having responded somewhat more at length than the Lord has determined in the Gospel. Then we taste of a mixture of milk and honey, administered (by the bishop); and from that day we abstain, during a whole week, from our daily bath" (*Cor. Mil* c. 3).—"Having gone forth, thereupon, out of the bath (of baptism), we are anointed with the holy unction, in conformity with the ancient ceremony, according to which priests were accustomed to be anointed to their office with oil from a flask. Then the hand (of the bishop) is imposed (upon us), asking, by means of the benediction, and inviting the Holy Spirit" (*Bapt.* c. 7, 8).

Trine Immersion, which consists of three distinct immersions,—one in the name of the Father, one in that of the Son, and one in that of the Holy Spirit,— performed upon the candidate in the one act of baptism, was now, and from this time forth, generally practiced in the churches both of the West and of the East.

Tertullian, in his treatise "Against Praxeas" (*Contra Praxeam*), assigns to Trine Immersion an apostolic origin. "Christ", he says (c. 26), "appointed baptism to be administered not in the name of one, but three, Father, Son, and Holy Ghost. Therefore, we are dipped (***tinguimur***) not once, but thrice, unto every person (of the Trinity) at the mention of each name."

This form of administering baptism,—which, whether apostolic or not, is, doubtless, allowable even now in practice,—was rigidly adhered to in the ancient Church at the end of this age, and during subsequent periods; until, in the seventh century, it was superseded in the churches the West, in accordance with the decision of Gregory the Great (†604) and with the decree of the fourth Council of Toledo (about 633), by a single immersion. In the churches of the East, the practice still continued; and, in common with other baptismal usages which arose at this period, has been preserved to this day in the so-called Greek Church, and among the Nestorians and other Christian sects of the East.

The ***laying on of hands*** (***cheirothesia***) performed even in apostolic days upon the recipient of the baptismal rite, had engrafted upon it, by the end of this period, a new significance. Through it as a medium, the Holy Spirit, it was thought, was specially conferred upon the baptized believer. Without it, therefore, the baptismal rite was supposed to be incomplete. To confer it became, in the churches of the West, the bishop's prerogative. Therefore, though the ceremony of baptism could be, and often was, performed by the presbyters or deacons of a church, the bishop alone, it was supposed in the West, could, by means of ***confirmation,*** as it was afterwards called, render the rite efficacious and complete. Baptism, consequently, except when administered by the bishop himself, became in the West a distinct act from confirmation, separated from it sometimes by a wide interval of time; and required the subsequent imposition of the hands of the bishop to make it perfect.—In the churches of the East, however, in which not the bishop only but also the baptizing presbyters could, and did, perform the ceremony the laying on hands, baptism and ***cheirothesia*** were not separated; but were performed upon the recipient at one and the same time.

§6. CORRUPTION: OF THE ACT OF BAPTISM.

Introduction, at the very close of the Period, of "Clinic" Affusion as Baptism— The Case of Novatian (251 A. D.) on Record—A "Clinic" not eligible to the Presbytership—Affusion of a "Clinic" Valid only in case of the Non-Recovery of the

Recipient—The Rite only Exceptional; and not performed upon all "Clinics"—Even the "Bed-ridden Sick" Immersed—Affusion as Baptism administered as an Exception for Ten Centuries—The "Greek Church" always the Advocate of Immersion—"Sprinkling" a Bar to its Union with the Roman Catholic Church—Brief Account of the Spread of Affusion as Baptism in the Western World.

At the very close of this period, a new rite was introduced, in the West, as a substitute in certain cases for Baptism. This was what is usually, but not very correctly, called "*Clinic Baptism*"; and was the ceremonial *affusion* (*pouring upon*) *of persons lying at the point of death.* Baptism was at this time usually administered to adults only after a long preparatory course of instruction; and as these *catechumens,* —who, as has been noticed, sometimes voluntarily deferred their reception of the ordinance on account of its supposed efficacy,—were sometimes taken ill, and threatened with death, during the term of their preparation, the ceremony of Baptism,—which had now come to be generally considered essential to salvation, because it was thought to be accompanied by, if not actually to effect in and of itself, the remission of all past sins,—could not be performed upon them, in their condition of illness, without danger of hastening their dissolution. Affusion, therefore, was substituted in its place; and this, under the circumstances, on account of the "pressing necessity" of the case, was considered valid baptism.

The first instance of the kind mentioned in ecclesiastical history is that of Novatian, a presbyter of Rome, who, not long previous to the year 251, when supposed to be in danger of death, was *perfused* (i. e. *poured upon, pericutheis*) as he lay on his couch. But, after Novatian's recovery, this substitution was not looked upon as valid; for Cornelius, the bishop of Rome in 251,—at which time Novatian was elected bishop in opposition to him by a party opposed to Cornelius,—expresses a doubt, in a letter of his, as to whether he had really received the rite of baptism; and his previous ordination as a presbyter, according to Eusebius (†340), been "opposed by all the clergy and many of the laity, as unlawful, because of his *clinic perfusion.*"

The case of Novatian is narrated by Cornelius in a letter to Fabius, bishop of Antioch; which is quoted by Eusebius in his Church History (bk. 6, c. 43). Cornelius says: "Being supposed at the point of death, having been perfused [(*pericutheis*), literally *poured around;* not *sprinkled,* as most translators of this passage in Eusebius have rendered] on the bed itself on which he was lying, he received (*regen-*

eration); if indeed it be right to say that such an one [that is, one so *perfused,* and not *immersed*] received it."

Such a clinic affusion, therefore, was considered valid, strictly speaking, only in case the recipient did not recover from his illness; for, as we learn from this example of Novatian's, no one who had been perfused, instead of being immersed, could receive clerical ordination; and, subsequently, the Council of Neo-Cæsarea (held in 315) expressly forbade, by its twelfth canon, that *clinics* should be "promoted to the rank of the presbytery".

Even clinics, however, were not always perfused. They were so treated only in cases of necessity; "when, for example",—as Dr. F. Brenner, a learned Roman Catholic historian who wrote early in the present century (1818) remarks, in his History of the Administration of Baptism (p. 15),—"no suitable place for immersion is (was) at hand, or when the candidate is (was) afflicted with a very severe sickness, rendering immersion impossible; *but otherwise even bed-ridden sick persons are (were) immersed.*"

H. Valesius, who edited Eusebius in the middle of the 17th century, remarks on the narrative respecting Novatian's perfusion, that "Rufinus [of Aquileia, who translated the Ecclesiastical History of Eusebius into Latin in the 4th century] rightly renders the Greek word (*pericutheis*) by *perfused* (*perfusus*); for clinics, *when they could not be immersed* by the priest, were only perfused with water."—"Such baptism," the learned Editor continues, "was held to be wanting in solemnity, and imperfect; because it seemed to be received not voluntarily, but through fear of death, by persons delirious and destitute of perception. Since,moreover, *baptism properly signifies immersion, a perfusion of this kind could scarcely be called baptism.*".

Thus was introduced in the West, for reasons which seemed good to some at that time,—but which, in truth, are wholly insufficient,—the practice of *affusion (pouring)*,—and, some centuries subsequently, *aspersion,* or *sprinkling,*—as a substitute, in certain cases, for the original and apostolic *immersion.*—Those persons, however, who had received only clinic affusion, were not, at this time, regarded as truly baptized; for the very name "clinics" (*couch-men*) was given them, as we learn from Cyprian, by way of reproach, instead of the honorable appellation of "Christians".—Nothing but a total immersion of the body in water was regarded, in this age, as Baptism; and, in all the ancient Church, the only persons who did not thus dip the whole body, were the Eunomians, a branch of the Arians, who, according to the testimony of Theodoret (†457), immersed, for peculiar reasons, only the upper part of the body as far as the breast.

The cases in which clinic affusion, or clinic sprinkling, was administered, continued, for at least ten centuries, to be exceptional; for, even so late as the time of Thomas Aquinas (†1274), *immersion* was the more common practice; and no ecclesiastical authority before the Council of Ravenna (1311) ventured to declare, as it did, "dipping or sprinkling indifferent".—"For thirteen hundred years", Brenner asserts (p. 306), "Baptism was generally and ordinarily an immersion of the person under water, and only in extraordinary cases a sprinkling or pouring with water: the latter [sprinkling or pouring], as a mode of baptism, was, moreover, called in question, aye, even forbidden".—This assertion is confirmed by the voice of ancient ecclesiastical history; and its truth is now generally admitted by all unprejudiced pædo-baptist church historiographers.

Christians of the East have never admitted the validity of perfusion and sprinkling as baptism. In ridicule of their brethren, of the West, they call them "sprinkled Christians". They have always practised immersion; and will allow nothing else to be the Christian ordinance. The subjoined testimony, of Alex, de Stourdza, a distinguished member of the Greek Churchy given in a volume published early in this century (1816), which is written in French, and entitled "Considerations on the Doctrine and Spirit of the Orthodox [Greek] Church" is conclusive on this point.

"The distinctive character of the institution of baptism, then, is *immersion,* (*baptisma*); which cannot be omitted without destroying the mysterious meaning of the sacrament, and without contradicting, at the same time, the etymological signification of the word which serves to designate it.—The Western [Romish] Church, therefore, has departed from the imitation of Jesus Christ: she has caused all the sublimity of the external sign to disappear: in short, she is guilty of an abuse of words and of ideas in practising *baptism by aspersion,* the mere announcement of which is a laughable contradiction. In point of fact, the verb (*baptizo*),—*immergo,* —has only one signification. Literally and always, it means *to plunge.* Baptism and immersion, therefore, are identical; and to speak of *baptism by aspersion,* is the same as if on should say *immersion by aspersion"* (p. 87).

Some centuries after the separation of the Western from the Oriental Church,—which took place in the middle of the 9th century,—an effort was made to re-unite the two at the papal session of Florence, in the year 1439. The Roman pontiff, Eugene IV., made use of rewards, threats, and promises, to bring the Greeks to his terms of accommodation; but in vain. Mark of Ephesus opposed the union; maintaining its impossibility, both before the Council and in an encyclical letter addressed to the bishops and churches of the Greeks, on the ground, among other reasons, that the baptism of the Latins was entirely different from that of the Greeks. And so, as we have seen, do the Greeks contend at the present day; still rejecting as invalid the aspersions and affusions practised by the Latins in all their churches but that of Milan.

France, according to the pædo-baptist Wall (History of Infant Baptism, pt. 2, ch. 9), "seems to have been the first country in the world where baptism by *affusion* was used ordinarily to persons in health, and in the public way of administering it". From France, where in 1160 "it was becoming an ordinary practice", *sprinkling* appears to have been introduced into Scotland; where, however, it was never practised in ordinary cases till after the Reformation. In Italy, Spain, and Germany, it made little progress before the 14th century. From Scotland, and from Switzerland (by means of the Calvinists) and Germany, sprinkling made its way, in turn, into England, in the reign of Elizabeth; but, though practised quite generally, it was not yet, in the ensuing reigns of James and Charles I., authorized by the rubric of the Established Church. To the Assembly of Presbyterian Divines, met at Westminster in 1643, is due the honor of having first, in England, publicly and solemnly "reformed the *font* into a *basin".*

The Council of Ravenna was the first ecclesiastical authority, as has been stated, which ventured to declare "dipping or sprinkling indifferent".—Stephen II., while an exile in France, having been driven from Rome in 753, is said indeed to have decided, to an application of the monks of Cressy in Brittany, that "in case of necessity, occasioned by the illness of an infant, it was lawful to baptize by *pouring* water on its head out of the hand or from a cup". The authenticity of account, however, is strenuously denied by some Catholics; and upon grounds apparently sufficient. If Stephen did so decide, he allowed *pouring,* we perceive, "only in case of imminent danger".

§7. NEW SUBJECTS OF THE BAPTISMAL RITE.

Rise of the Baptism of Children in North Africa (Carthage and Alexandria) as a Consequence of the Doctrine of Baptismal Regeneration—Baptism of Children first Mentioned by Tertullian, as an Opponent of the Practice—The Rite mentioned by Origen—These Children not Infants—Misunderstanding of Christ's Words, "Suffer the [Little] Children, etc".—Explanation of their Real Meaning—Testimony of the Alexandrian Church Text Book—Infant Baptism, properly so called, first Mentioned by Cyprian—Sanctioned at Carthage in 252 A. D.—The Practice known yet only in North Africa—Its Progress in other Countries, Slow—Not generally Established even in the Beginning of the Fifth Century.

The belief that Baptism is a saving ordinance, on the ground that it washes away all sins which have been previously committed by its recipient,—that is, all personal transgressions,—was almost universal in the Church during the greater part of this period; but it was not until towards the close of it, that there was superadded to this doctrine, in some of the African churches, the dogma that baptism also cleanses from original or inherited sin. The first patristic writings in which this doctrine seems to be advocated are those of the learned Origen, of the church in Alexandria, in the first half of the third century; but the most ardent supporter of the dogma, during this period, was Cyprian (245?258), bishop of Carthage, in North Africa. From this erroneous view of the intent and efficacy of baptism there had originated, among the African churches, by the time of Origen (203—254), a mischievous and corrupting application of the baptismal ordinance. This was the *Baptism of Children;* and, by the time of Cyprian, the baptism even of *unconscious Infants.*

The first mention in any ecclesiastical writer of the baptism of any other than a grown person, is found in the treatise of Tertullian "On Baptism" (c. 18), written about 200 A. D. , first of all the Fathers, speaks of the baptism of *children;* and he does so expressly *to oppose* the practice. "It is more advantageous", he says, "to postpone baptism, according to the condition and disposition of each individual, as well as in reference to his age; but *especially* so in the case of *children (parvuli).* For where is the necessity of placing the sponsors in danger; who may be prevented by death from performing their promises, or may be deceived by the breaking out of an evil disposition? It is true our Lord said, 'Forbid them not to come unto me'. Let them come, then, when they arrive at the age of puberty; let them come when they begin to learn, and when they are taught to whom they are coming: let them come when they are able to know Christ . . . . . . They who attach to baptism its true importance, will fear over-haste rather than delay. Perfect faith is sure of salvation."

In the time of Tertullian, then, the baptism of children was known in the church at Carthage. Somewhat later, Origen testifies to the existence of the practice in the church at Alexandria; and asserts expressly that children were baptized in accordance with an apostolic tradition. But this assertion of an apostolic tradition in favor of the ceremony, "can not, in this century", as Neander truthfully observes, "be considered of any great weight; because men were at that time so much inclined to deduce the ordinances which they thought of great importance, from the Apostles; and, besides this, there were many partition walls between this age and the apostolic, which prevented a free insight into that period".

The passage in which Origen bears this testimony to the baptism of children in his time, occurs in the fifth book of his Commentary on Romans, according to the Latin translation of Rufinus (which was made about the year 400, and is known to contain additions to the original Greek of Origen); and the word there used is ***parvuli***, —a, term which does not mean ***infants,*** as is generally assumed, but ***young growing children,*** "from about six to ten years old", such as those spoken of in the Gospels as brought to our Lord for his blessing. The same word, as has been seen, is used in the passage cited from Tertullian. It is found also in that memorable passage of Irenæus, occurring in his treatise "Against Heretics" (II. c. 22. §4), which was once thought quite generally to refer to infant baptism; and which is still supposed to have allusion to that rite by those among pædo-baptist controversialists who have not examined the passage in the original. The passage, however, is now given up by the best informed among the pædo-baptists; and is supposed by the best biblical critics not to refer to baptism in any sense, much less to the baptism of infants. Here in Irenæus, the term (***parvuli***) is expressly contrasted with ***infantes*** (***infants***) and ***pueri*** (***boys***) in such a way that there can possibly be no mistake as to its meaning. "He came", Irenæus says, speaking of Christ, "to save all persons by himself; all, I say, who are regenerated [i. e ***redeemed,*** not ***baptized***] by him unto God, ***infants*** (*infantes*), and *children,* (*parvuli*) and *boys* (*pueri*), and young men, and old men. Therefore, he went through every age of life," etc. Irenæus expresses here the beautiful idea that Jesus is the redeemer of man in every stage of his existence, from infancy to old age; and that, in order to become such, he passed himself through every stage of human life. Baptism is alluded to in no manner whatever.

Tertullian, consequently, is the first Christian writer who speaks of the baptism of children; and he, as well as Origen, refers, unquestionably, to the baptism of *young growing children,* and not to that of *infants.*

If there be any doubt of the correctness of the interpretation here given to these noteworthy passages in Tertullian and Origen, it will be set at rest by the explicit testimony of the Church Text Book used in Alexandria in the time of Origen, himself an Alexandrian. From this Text Book may be learned what was considered apostolic tradition on this point in the church at Alexandria; and what, therefore, *must* be the import of the expressions used by its presbyter Origen. The word employed by Origen (*parvuli*) shows that *children,* not *infants,* are meant; and the representation of the Text Book proves that no other interpretation of his expressions is admissible. "The Text Book", Bunsen remarks in his work already quoted from, on Hippolytus, "speaks of those who *go down* with the other catechumens into the baptismal bath, but are not yet in a state to make the *proper* responses; in that case, the parents are bound to do it for them. This was undoubtedly the apostolic practice to which Origen refers; for it was to the church of Alexandria that he particularly belonged.—In this ordinance, the whole arrangement seems to be *exceptional one;* and so it is in Origen, for he says, 'the little ones also'. "

In instituting pædo-baptisin in this sense, that is, the baptism of young growing children,—children not yet old enough to make "the *proper* responses" to the baptismal Confession of Faith,—the church in Alexandria proceeded, doubtless, upon an incorrect understanding, or at least upon an unauthorized application, of those well-known words of our Lord, "Suffer *the* [little] children to come unto me, and forbid them not; for such is the kingdom of heaven." These words are expressly referred to by Origen, when treating on this subject. And they are referred to also by Tertullian; and evidently with the direct intention of refuting the incorrect interpretation of them which was beginning to spread at the time when he wrote his work "On Baptism".

A like misunderstanding of these words of our Lord has prevailed in modern times. The Reformers appealed to them in justification of infant baptism; and they are even cited now-a-days to prove the validity of that ceremony. Among those who read only the English Scriptures, this misunderstanding is fostered by an erroneous rendering of the most important part of our Lord's expression.

The narrative of the blessing of the children is given in the first three Gospels (Matt. 19: 13-15, Mark 10: 13–16, Luke 18: 15–17); and in two of them, Matthew and Luke, the English Version, omitting the Article, has, "Suffer little children", etc., instead of "Suffer *the* [little] children", etc. The Greek, in every place, has *to paidia;* "the children". The omission of the Article in translating makes a very essential difference in the sense of the expression; for it converts it from *a specific direction,* referring only to those particular children then presented to Christ, *to a general precept* applicable to all children. The command of Jesus was, that those children whom his disciples were keeping away, should come to him; and, when they had come, he gave them his blessing. He did not make them members of his visible Church; nor did he hint that they, or any other children, could in any way become such, before they were able to exercise an intelligent faith in him as the promised Messiah.

It is, moreover, to be noted respecting our English rendering of these passages in the Gospels, that (*ta paidia*) does not mean "the *little* children". So to translate it, is to assume the point in dispute. The Greek (*paidion*) means simply *a child.* Though the term is sometimes applied to a *little* child, or *infant,* usually, and properly, it designates a child between the ages of from four to ten or twelve. And so it means in the passages before us; in all of which the Vulgate renders by *parvuli,* a term quite distinct in signification from the Latin *infantes* (infants).

The Greek for *infants,* or *babes,* is usually (*brephe*); but even this word is sometimes applied to children that are not infants. Thus, Luke, in his narrative of this transaction, once uses the term (v. 15) in the same way as—rendered in our Version by "*infants*". Here, however, the fact that Luke, in all other places in the passage, employs the word, as is done in every case in Matthew and Mark, shows that children older than infants are meant; just as, in 2 Tim. 3: 15, we read of Timothy, that "from a *child*" he was *"acquainted with the Scriptures";* where *brephos* quite clearly does not mean a babe, or *infant.*[13]

The manner in which the Evangelists narrate this transaction, proves, beyond question, that the children spoken of were not infants; but young growing children, capable, not only of walking, but of understanding speech. All three of the Evangelists represent our Lord as saying "forbid them not to *come"* [(*eithein*), (*erchesthai*)],—not, to be *brought,* which idea would have been expressed by (*prosenecthenai*),—evidently implying that the children could walk. And even more than this is said; for Luke,—the very Evangelist who uses *brepe* in one place, as we have seen,—say's expressly, "Jesus called [(*proskalesamenos*), *having called;* showing that the children are addressed in person] them unto him."[14]

Infant Baptism, properly so called, is first mentioned and defended by Cyprian of Carthage, in the middle of the third century; he being "the first Father who", to use the words of an eminent pædo-baptist, "impelled by a fanatical enthusiasm, and assisted by a bad interpretation of the Old Testament, established it as a principle."

---

13   The word *brephos* is applied in a number of places in the Greek Classics to children capable of intelligent action. Theocritus (who flourished 272 B. C.) of a boy who was old enough to understand what his mother was saying about his father (Idyl 15, 1. 14). Moschus (fl. 154 B. C.) applies it to the "runaway'" Cupid (Idyl 1, 1. 11). Anacreon (fl. 559 B. C.) does the same, several times, in his Ode to Eros (Ode 4). See also Lucian, Toxaris, 26; and the Palatine Anthology, 7, 632. Other examples might be cited. For those here given, the Author is indebted to the research of his friend, Geo. Wyndham, Esq., of New Orleans.

14   The received Version, moreover, represents Mark as saying that our Lord "took them [the children] up in his arms, put his hands upon them, and blessed them" (v. 16). How he could hold the children in his arms, and at the same time "put his *hands* upon them", is rather, difficult to conceive. Jesus did not, in fact, take them up in his arms at all, but merely *embraced* them. The Greek word here rendered "*took up in his arms"*, (*enagkatisamenos*), ought to be translated, both here and in Mark 9: 36, by *having embraced,* or *when he had embraced,* correspondent with the *complexus esset* and *complexans* of the Vulgate.—Had our Lord taken the children up into his arms, we should have had some such expression as this, (cp, Luke 2: 28).

Cyprian, and some other African bishops, his contemporaries, "were the first", as Bunsen remarks, "who viewed baptism in the light of a washing away of the universal sinfulness of human nature, and connected this idea with the ordinance of the Old Testament circumcision." Since they thought that original hereditary sin, just as much as actual personal transgression, was washed away, and remitted, in baptism, it was quite natural for them to advocate the administration of that ordinance, as they did, to new-born and unconscious children.

Thus originated in North Africa, Infant Baptism proper; somewhere about the middle of the third century, one hundred and fifty years after the last Apostle had left the scene of his earthly labors. In the year 252, the new ceremony was sanctioned by a Council of sixty-six bishops in Carthage; Cyprian being the leader and the directing spirit of the Council.

Only in North Africa, however, in the churches under the influence of Carthage and its bishop, was this perversion of the baptismal ordinance practised, at any time, during the whole period now under consideration. No mention is made of its being even known elsewhere; not in Asia Minor; not in Greece; not in Rome, nor in any of the other churches of the West.

The progress of the new rite from Africa,—where, from the first, it was, by a legitimate theoretical inference, associated in practice with *infant communion,*—was slow; and it spread into other countries only by degrees. In *theory,* its necessity was, within something over a century, quite generally allowed; but, in *practice,* it became by no means general, even among "the orthodox", until after the time of Chrysostom (†407) and Augustine (†430). Many Christians, distinguished in Church or State, who lived in and about the fourth century, were not baptized until after they had reached the years of manhood. Among these were the ecclesiastics Ambrose, Jerome, Augustine, Chrysostom, Basil, and Gregory Nazianzen; and the Emperors Constantine, Constantius, Valentinian, Gratian, and Theodosius. This shows that the rite was not yet, in the beginning of the fifth century, generally established, even among those who admitted its abstract necessity. The same fact is attested by baptismal rituals of the period, the language of which presupposes that adults were the baptized; by the canons of several Councils; and by the existence of discourses of the Fathers addressed to persons deferring their baptism.

The precise time of the general introduction and practice of Infant Baptism, can not be determined. It never, at any time, became universal. Baptists still lived, and Baptist practices still existed, to a greater or less extent, in the Christian world.—To trace the history of these, shall be the object of future volumes of this "History of the Baptists, and of Baptist Principles and Practices".

§8. "TRACES" OF INFANT BAPTISM IN THE FATHERS.

The most Eminent pædo-baptist Scholars find no Trace of Infant Baptism before the Time of Tertullian—Such a Rite not alluded to in the "Apostolic Fathers"—The "Apostolic Fathers", in this respect, all Baptists—The Single Passage from Justin Martyr Examined and Interpreted—Justin knows only Adult Baptism—The Single Passage from Irenæus Examined and Interpreted—Does not countenance Infant Baptism—Testimony of Dr. Chase, and of the German Critics—Tertullian's Child Baptism not Infant Baptism—The Passages in Origen Examined—Can not be cited in favor of pædo-baptism—Origen knows only the Baptism of Believers—Dr. Chase's Examination of the Passages in Origen—Baptism of Infants first mentioned and defended by Cyprian—The Rite "utterly unknown in the Early Church"—The Primitive Church, for three Centuries, Baptist.

It was remarked, in the previous section, that "the first mention in any ecclesiastical writer of the baptism of any other than a grown person, is found in the treatises of Tertullian on Baptism (c. 18)." The leading critics and theologians of the present day, even among those who favor infant baptism, concede that such a rite is not mentioned in any of the Fathers before Tertullian; and very few pædo-baptists of any pretensions to scholarship, contend, in this age of biblical criticism, that such an ordinance is spoken of in any patristic writing anterior to the time of Irenæus. There are yet some pædo-baptist authors in this country, however, and some in England,—men distinguished for zeal rather than for critical learning,—who, following the authority of Dr. William Wall, whose "History of Infant Baptism" (published first in 1705) "has", to use the words of Prof. Ripley, "long been the storehouse of historical arguments for English and American advocates of infant baptism", assert, even now-a-days, that pædo-baptism is not only expressly mentioned in Irenæus, and in Justin Martyr, but even alluded to in the writings of the "Apostolic Fathers"; and thus, as they think, they "trace back the custom of baptizing infants to the age of the Apostles". It may not be amiss, therefore, in order to correct this error, to call attention briefly to the passages of the Fathers in which, according to this opinion, infant baptism is either mentioned or implied.

A short sketch of the Apostolic Fathers and of their writings, has been given already in another chapter of the present treatise. Not a single passage can be found in any of their extant productions which recognizes, or in any way alludes to, the baptism of any others than those capable of exercising faith in Christ. All their writings,—which reach down to about 150 A. D.,—are as free as the New Testament itself from allusion to any other than the normal baptism of believers. "The darkness of Egypt", it has been well said by Prof. Ripley, "was not more destitute of a cheering beam of light, than is the historical period embraced by the Apostolical Fathers destitute of evidence that infant baptism then existed."

The instances in which Baptism is mentioned in the Apostolic Fathers have been carefully collected by Dr. Ripley, and ably exhibited by him in an Article in the Christian Review for Oct., 1851 (Vol. xvi. pp. 508-511). Their testimony is all on the side of the Baptists.—*Barnabas,* where he speaks of the Christian ordinance (Epist. §11), says: "We descend into the water laden with sins and corruption, and ascend bearing fruit, having in the heart the fear [towards God] and in the spirit the hope towards Jesus;" which, obviously, can be said of believers alone.—*Hermas,* in his Pastor (Shepherd), speaks several times of baptism; but alludes in no way to its being administered to infants. He is a firm believer in the necessity of the rite; and thinks, extravagantly enough, that the Apostles, after their death, preached the Gospel, and baptized the worthies of the Old Testament, in the world of departed spirits.—*Clement* of Rome, in his Epistle to the Corinthians, does not allude to baptism at all. And yet he enjoins upon the brethren in Corinth, that they should give their children "instruction in Christ" (§21. cp. Eph. 6: 4). The second so-called Epistle of Clement,—which, however, was not written by that Father, but by a much later hand,—speaks, in two or three places, of the ordinance; but always in such a way as to indicate a personal recognition, on the part of the recipient, "of the duty and purpose to lead a righteous life".—*Ignatius* mentions baptism in his Epistle to the Ephesians (§18), in that to the Smyrneans (§§1, 8), and in that to Poly carp (§6); but, in every instance, in such a manner that the idea of infant baptism is manifestly altogether excluded.—*Polycarp,* in his Epistle the Philippians, makes no allusion at all to the Christian ordinance.

Passing out of the age of the "Fathers Apostolic", we come to that of the earlier Church Fathers, which extends from about 150 A. D. death of Origen, 254 A. D. already been seen how far any of these Fathers allow the baptism of others besides believers. They do not, in fact, recognize any other baptism at all. It is necessary, however, to examine the representations of four among them a little more in detail. These four are Justin Martyr, Irenæus, Tertullian, and Origen; each of whom has been quoted in favor of pædo-baptism by the opponents of the Baptists in the baptismal controversy.

Justin Martyr is now given up by almost all pædo-baptist scholars; but some controversialists refer still in support of infant baptism to a passage in his First Apology (§15), in which he has the following: "Many men and many women, sixty and seventy years old, who, from children (**ek paidon**), have been disciples (**emath-eteuthesan**) of Christ, preserve their continence." Justin, however, only says here that persons of both sexes became disciples in early life. The Greek verb which he employs,—which is the same as that used by our Lord in the commission (rendered in the English Version by "teach"),—implies the conscious and intelligent act of becoming a disciple. It does not necessarily include the idea of being baptized; and, even if it does, the verb must, from its own intrinsic meaning, refer only to such as have will and intelligence sufficient to become disciples. The expression "*from children*" (**ek paidon**) is indicative, as usual elsewhere, not of the period of infancy, but of that of childhood or youth. Besides all this, Justin, in giving his account of Baptism (elsewhere quoted from), "relates that *only those who believe* the things that are taught, so as to be persuaded that they can live in a Christian manner, are brought to baptism".

Semisch, a Lutheran clergyman, and, of course, a pædo-baptist, who has written a critical monograph on the Life and Works of Justin, says, in his second volume (p. 334), as quoted by Ripley: "Whenever Justin refers to baptism, *adults* appear as the objects to whom the sacred rite is administered. *Of an infant baptism he knows nothing.* The traces of it which some persons believe they have detected in his writings, are groundless fancies, artificially produced." To the same effect speaks Matthies in his able prize Essay entitled *Baptismatis Expositio* (p. 187). The object of this Apology of Justin's was to give a full account of the usages and practices of Christianity in his day. It is inconceivable, therefore, that, had infant baptism been known and practised in his time, he should not have mentioned its existence. And this would be the more astonishing, since, by so doing, he might have triumphantly refuted a charge then current among the heathen,—the grossest and vilest ever brought against the religion of Jesus,—that Christians, Thyestes-like, were wont to banquet upon the flesh of children.

There is a passage in Irenæus which is supposed by some to refer to the baptism of infants. It occurs in his treatise against the Heretics; and has been previously quoted in this work, and made a subject of comment. The question here is one purely of literary criticism; the turning-point being, what is meant by the phrase ***renascuntur in Deum,*** "are regenerated unto God". It used to be thought quite generally,—as by Wall, Bingham, and Schrœckh,?it is yet contended by some, that the phrase refers to baptism. If it does, infant baptism is unquestionably alluded to by Irenaeus; for he says, refering to Christ, "He came to save all persons by himself; all, I say, who are regenerated (***renascuntur***) by him unto God; infants, and children, and boys, and young me, and old men." An impartial investigation of the passage and its context, however, will prove that the idea of baptism is wholly excluded. Rev. Dr. Chase, who has examined the entire passage with scrupulous care,—having, with this end in view, "read and re-read every page of all the extant works of Irenæus",—has rightly conceived and happily expressed its real meaning.—"According to Irenæus", he says (as referred to below), "Christ, in becoming incarnate, and thus assuming his mediatorial work, brought the human family into a new relation, under himself, and placed them in a condition in which they can be saved.—In this sense, he is the Saviour of all. He restored them, or summed them up anew, in himself. He became, so to speak, a second Adam, regenerator of mankind. Through him they are 'regenerated unto God'; per eum renascuntur in Deum."

An able Article on this passage in Irenæus, from the pen of Rev. Dr. Chase, appears in the Bib. Sacra and Theol. Review for Nov., 1849 (Vol. vi. pp. 646–656). The view which the author takes, corresponds, as he afterwards found, with that advocated by some of the most distinguished biblical critics of Germany,—men who, though pædo-baptists in practice, speak, as do almost all the German Theologians, "with the utmost freeness of the introduction of infant baptism at a date subsequent to that of the Apostles". Baumgarten-Crusius, a name that stands high in theological literature, says in his History of Doctrines (Dogmengeschichte), p. 1209: "The celebrated passage in Irenæus (11. 22. 4) is not to be used in favor of infant baptism." Hagenbach, who is better known among us in America, remarks in his History of Doctrines, p. 178 (2d edit.): "It [this passage] merely expresses the beautiful idea that Jesus was Redeemer *in* every stage of life, and *for* every stage of life; but it does not say that he became Redeemer for children *by water baptism;* unless the term *renasci* [to be regenerated] be interpreted by an arbitrary petitio principii to refer to baptism." To the same effect speak Winer, Starck, Rossler, Münscher, Von Cöln, Krabbe, Bötringer, etc.

Down to the time of Tertullian, then, we find no mention in any one of the Church Fathers of a baptism administered to any other than a person capable of exercising, and actually exercising, faith in Christ as the promised Messiah. Tertullian, however, as has been elsewhere seen, speaks of a baptism performed upon children. Yet, these children are not *infants,* but children of such an age as to be able to understand something of Christ; children possessing intelligence, but not sufficiently "instructed and established in the principles of piety". They are capable of being taught; but have not been *fully* and *properly* taught. "Tertullian's opposition", Bunsen says, "is to the baptism of young, growing children: he does not say a word about new-born infants." He declares against baptizing children before they really and fully "know Christ". The practice which he opposes, was, as Neander (who, however, calls it infant baptism) truthfully says in his Spirit of Tertullian (p. 207), "certainly not a generally prevailing practice; and was not yet regarded as an apostolical institution, On the contrary, as the assertions of Tertullian render in the highest degree probable, it had just begun to spread, and was therefore regarded by many as an innovation."

Origen, the next Father, in the order of time, after Tertullian and Clement of Alexandria, also speaks, as has been noticed, of the baptism of children. In three different places in his works mention is made of the baptism of *parvuli* (children),—a word which has been generally, but incorrectly, understood to refer to *infants.* These passages are 1.) from his Homily VIII. on Leviticus (ch. 12: 1-8), as it has come to us in the Latin translation of Rufinus; 2.) from his Homily XIV. on Luke (ch. 2: 21–24), as translated by Jerome; 3.) from his Commentary on Romans (bk. v. 9), as translated by Rufinus. The original Greek of Origen in these passages is not extant; and the renderings of Rufinus and Jerome are justly liable to suspicion; for each altered Origen freely, subtracting and largely adding, in his translation of the original into Latin. The work of neither, indeed, is, strictly speaking, a translation at all; but is, as Redepenning justly observes, "intermediate between a translation and a treatise; a reproduction adapted to the views and wants of the later age [beginning of the fifth century] in which it was prepared".

The passages in question certainly have the air and appearance of additions to the original Greek by the hands of Rufinus and Jerome. But, even if we have here the words of Origen himself, it does not follow that infants are the subjects of allusion. It has been already shown that infants are not, in all probability, referred to, but young growing children. Such is the meaning of the term *parvuli,* it is certain, in the passage which has been cited from Irenæus; and such is, most likely, its signification in the passage from Tertullian; as it is, beyond a question, in some other places in Origen himself. Origen, speaking for himself, even indirectly opposes infant baptism; for other passages in his writings show that, in his view, only the instructed in Christianity should be baptized.

An elaborate and thorough Article on the "Testimony of Origen respecting the Baptism of Children", written by the Rev. Dr. Chase, appears in the Christian Review for April, 1854 (Vol. xix., pp. 180?208). The learned and pains-taking Author establishes, by irresistible proofs, the truth of the opinion that Origen knows nothing of *infant* baptism properly speak; but, at the most, only of the baptism of children old enough to exercise faith in Christ and to be instructed in the truths of the Gospel. Not to mention other passages, a single one in his work against Celsus (bk. iii., c. 59) will set the whole question at rest. Celsus had objected to Christianity, that it invited every body,—"the sinner", "the unintelligent", "the *mere child"* (*nepios*), every "miserable and contemptible creature",—into the kingdom of God. The Alexandrian Theologian replies: "We exhort sinners to come to the instruction that teaches them not to sin; and the unintelligent to come to that which produces in them understanding; and *the little children* (*nepioi*) *to rise in elevation of thought unto the man* . . . . And when those the exhorted that *make progress show that they have been cleansed by the word, and, as much as possible, have lived a better life,* THEN *we invite them to be initiated among us. "*

One feels impelled just here to exclaim with Dr. Chase, "We would render devout thanks to God, that, under his good and ever watchful providence, this passage has been preserved from the ravages of time. Here it stands, an authentic record in the original Greek. Henceforth, let its light shine on what has been a much obscured place in ecclesiastical antiquity."

Origen, it is clear, can not be longer quoted in favor of infant baptism. The three passages which seem to allude to it, must either be interpreted in harmony with that which has been cited from his book against Celsus, or must be admitted to be interpolations made by Rufinus and Jerome. According to Origen himself, "*little children*", as well as others, are, before they receive baptism, "to be taught, and to give evidence of having duly heeded the voice of Christian instruction".

It has been seen, in this examination of the alleged "Trace of Infant Baptism in the Fathers", that such a rite is not mentioned, nor even alluded to in any manner, in the so-called "Apostolic Fathers". It has been established, furthermore, that the only passage in Justin Martyr which is ever cited in favor of the existence of pædo-baptism in his day, does not, of necessity, include the idea of baptism; and if it does, it is the baptism of those who are old enough to become "disciples", and not, most assuredly, the baptism of unconscious infants. It has been shown, moreover, that the pædo-baptist proof-text from Irenæus must be surrendered by all, as it has been by many, as not referring to baptism in any sense; and it has been shown that Tertullian and Origen, when they speak of the baptism of children, give no countenance whatever to the idea of pædo-baptism as understood and practised in modern times.

Cyprian, however, does testify in favor of infant baptism proper; but Cyprian wrote in the middle-of the third century. Until, his time, the early Church knows nothing of the baptism of infants. "Pædo-baptism" in the modern sense", remarks the learned and candid Bunsen (Hippolytus, vol. iii, p. 179), "meaning thereby the baptism of new-born infants, with the vicarious promises of parents and sponsors [and, of course, much less *without* such "vicarious promises"] was *utterly unknown* in the early Church, not only down to the end of the second, but indeed *to the middle of the third* century . . . . . Cyprian being the first Father who, impelled by a fanatical enthusiasm, and assisted by a bad interpretation of the Old Testament, established it as a principle."

The early Church, from the time of Christ and the Apostles down to the middle of the third century, knew no other baptism than the baptism of believers, administered to the recipient on the profession of his faith in Jesus as the Messiah and the Son of God. During the same period, and for centuries later, it acknowledged only one act as baptism; and that act was the immersion in water of the body of the candidate,—whereby he was initiated into the visible Church Apostolic and Universal. In these two cardinal principles of Gospel usage, the Church of the first three centuries was thoroughly Baptist. And these are the very principles which are at this day, and have been in all its history, the distinctive doctrines of the Baptist denomination. Based upon the teachings of the New Testament, and upheld by the universal practice of the primitive Church for a century and a half after the last Apostle had gone to his rest, they must live for ever, unshaken by the assaults of misbelief and infidelity; and, towering up in beauty and grandeur, uninjured amid the quarrels and dissensions of a non-primitive Christianity, and pure amid its errors and corruptions, they must stand forth in their simple majesty in every age, usages and principles of the Apostolic "Church of the living God, the pillar and ground of the Truth".

CHAPTER IV.
THE LIFE, EXTERNAL AND INTERNAL, OF THE EARLY BAPTISTS.

§1. THE FAITH OF THE ANCIENT CHURCH.

Jesus or the Apostles, not Authors of a Strict Dogmatic Theology—Faith of the Early Baptists Simple; based on Christian Facts, rather than Doctrines—The "Rule of Faith"—The New Testament and the Articles of Christian Belief—New Testament Scriptures, the Record of the Faith and Doctrines of the Church—Jesus of Nazareth, the Central-point of Christian Faith and Hope.

In a previous section, a sketch has been given of the "speculative doctrines of the Apostolic Church and of the Church Fathers". But little, however, has yet been said of the practical doctrines of the Early Church; those doctrines which intertwined themselves with the whole life of believers, and prompted them to every word and action. Jesus, as has been intimated, did not teach a Dogmatic Theology; but only imparted, in a fragmentary form, the eternal truths of the religion of Heaven. The Apostles, particularly Paul and John, formed indeed a system of doctrines; but not a sharply-defined and logical system like that of the Schoolmen of the middle ages, and those of the Schools of Theology of our day. It was long, however, before believers at large began to build up the doctrines of Christianity in a connected and systematic manner. At first, they were satisfied with the simple confession that Jesus of Nazareth is the Christ, that he is the Messiah promised by the prophets, and that he is the Son of God and the Saviour of the world. Whoever received these simple truths in honesty of heart, and, having openly confessed his belief in them, at his baptism, afterwards conformed to their requirements in his life, he was a Christian.

The baptismal confession of faith related rather to the facts than to the speculative doctrines of Christianity. He who uttered it professed his belief, in words few and simple, in God, the Father, Creator of heaven and earth; in Jesus Christ, as the Son of God; in the Holy Ghost, as the vivifier of the Church; in the forgiveness of sins through Christ, the resurrection of the body and the life everlasting. At a later period, early in the second century, preparatory instruction, in some of the leading doctrines of Christianity, was given to candidates for baptism; and hence arose in Alexandria, in which city also Theology was first cultivated as a science, the catechumenate, or preparatory school, for young believers who were not yet, as was thought, sufficiently enlightened in the truths of the Christian religion to be admitted, by baptism, into the full fellowship of the faithful.

It was quite necessary in the early days of Christianity, that there should be a well understood outline of Christian doctrine, which should constitute a "rule of faith"; for at this period the Holy Scriptures of the New Testament did not exist in a collected form, and had by no means found their way into the whole of Christendom. Christianity was propagated in that age by the verbal preaching of the Word, not by the circulation of the Scriptures. The melting story of Jesus and the resurrection was told by the living voice, and not by pen, and ink, and paper.

The New Testament itself arose out of the necessities of the Church; and to understand it fully, we, in this day, must know what those necessities were. Early Christianity had and knew no religious text-book other than the Scriptures of the Old Testament. The Epistles of Paul, the first written of the books of the New Testament, grew out of the peculiar wants of churches which he had founded, or instructed; and the Gospels themselves, indispensable as they are in this age, were written years after the Lord's death, to keep alive his memory forever in the world. The hand of God was in this all. He raised up the early Church; and He prepared men in it, who, moved and guided by the Spirit, should give to all men, in a fixed and permanent form, the narrative of Jesus and redeeming love. Verbal tradition, kept pure by the providence of God, first instructed the Church, and then holy men, directed by the Spirit, recorded that tradition in the Gospels and Epistles of the New Testament. The Church was founded on the living Word of God; and this Word was afterwards recorded by competent and heaven-inspired penmen, in indelible characters, in the Scriptures of the New Covenant of mercy and love.—This, preserved, under God, by the early Church, has come down to us uncorrupted and truthful; telling to us from Apostolic or heaven-guided pens, if not from Apostolic lips, the wondrous story of redemption.

The primitive Christians believed in a God, uncreated, invisible, and eternal; a God, who is the Father of all things, who has made Himself visible to men in Jesus Christ, His Son, and who works in believers by the power of the Holy Ghost. This was the ground-doctrine of their faith. Christ was their Redeemer, their Sanctifier, and the source of all their blessings, temporal as well as spiritual. By his death, He freed them from the condemnation of the law; by His intercession, and the workings of the Holy Spirit, He purified and preserved them from sin; and by His mighty power over all things, He raised them from the grave, and conveyed them to eternal glory. Positive and fixed rules of Faith, they had few; but evidences and fruits of Faith, they had many. Faith and hope in Jesus as the Son of God, as the Saviour of the world, and as the Lord of the Kingdom of Heaven, was the root and kernel of their Christian life; the star which led them on to life eternal. Their hearts were directed to Him; from Him, when persecuted, they looked for help and strength; and from Him they expected the perfection of the Church, and victory over every foe. Burning with love, they offered their hearts to Him: they gave all to Him, because in Him and by Him they firmly expected to attain everlasting joy and felicity. Their "lives were hid with Christ in God".

§2. THE SPIRITUAL GIFTS OF THE PRIMITIVE BAPTISTS.

Special Gifts of the Spirit necessary in the Early Church—Their Influence contrasted with that of Christian Example—The Miracle-working Power conveyed by "the Gift of the Holy Ghost"—Time of its Continuance in the Church—Exerted, probably, after the Death of the Apostles—Died away by Degrees—Outward

"Signs" and "Wonders" not the most Striking Miracles of Ancient Christianity—The Church, a Standing and Perpetual Miracle—Success of Christianity the greatest Wonder—Language of Dr. Hagenbach on this Topic.

Christianity is, and has proved itself to be, "not merely a theory, nor an emotion, nor a collection of moral precepts and actions; but life in the deepest and most comprehensive sense". The community founded by Jesus, and fully established "on the day of Pentecost," was meant to be a world-renewing community; "the basis of every true advance in morality, science, art, social life and outward civilization, as well as the spring of all great events in later history". At first, when it was weak, and just beginning its attacks upon the strongholds of sin, God, through the Spirit, conferred upon the Church special powers or *charisms.* Not the Apostles only, but the disciples at large, were, on the day of Pentecost, endowed with power "to speak with tongues"; and they were made able, through faith in Jesus, to perform works of unusual and even miraculous might. This power of working "signs and wonders" was certainly found, and certainly used, in the Church of Apostolic times. Believers in that age could and did perform miracles; and they who, witnessing them, were converted to Christ, were compelled to cry out in the words of the Psalmist, "This is the Lord's doing; it is marvellous in our eyes."

And yet, after all, even in that day of miracle-working, men were brought to Christ, as they are now, rather by the force of the truth commending itself to their consciences, and by seeing in those who already believed "the fruits of the spirit". They saw that the spirit of Christianity is a spirit of gentleness and love; giving peace to the mind, and waking up in the soul hope and joy in the Holy Ghost. Beholding, they first wondered, then adored; and thus the religion of Jesus, exemplified in the lives of its professors, was spread far and wide in the world; and many, embracing it, laid hold on eternal life.

The "Gift of the Holy Ghost" which was granted to believers, in Apostolic times, at their baptism, or, subsequently, on the imposition of the hands of an Apostle, conferred, in some instances at least, the power of "speaking with tongues" and of working miracles. During our Lord's personal ministry, not only "the twelve", but the "seventy" disciples also, performed miracles in his name, and by his authority. In the same way, after the full establishment of the Church, other Christians besides the Apostles were endowed with miracle-working gifts. The writings of the

New Testament bear express testimony to this fact; and, while they do so, give no hint that this miracle-working power either had ceased, or was destined to cease, in the Church. Yet this Christian charism *has* departed from the Church; or, at least, has not manifested itself for many centuries. When, then, did it disappear? At what period did "the gift of the Holy Ghost" cease to operate in the Church by "miracles of power" over outward physical nature, and confine itself to the working of inward spiritual miracles of grace?

This question is more easily asked than answered. That miracle-working did not at once and wholly pass away with the Apostolic Age, seems too well attested to be denied. The existence and the exercise of the power, at least in the first part of the period succeeding that of the Apostles, are testified to by many credible Christian witnesses, ?"grave men, fair and honest, some of them philosophers; men who lived in different countries, and related not what they *heard,* but what they *saw,* calling on God to witness the truth of their declarations". And this "unanimous and concordant testimony of the ancient writers" is not denied, but admitted, by heathen opponents of Christianity living at the time; who would certainly, had they been able, have exposed the falsity of the claims set up by the new and hated religion of the despised Nazarene. To suppose that the miraculous gifts of the Holy Spirit ceased to operate at once, and immediately, on the death of the Apostles, is contrary to the express testimony of credible witnesses, and contrary to all historic analogy. They rather disappeared gradually, as the Church was brought more and more under regular and settled training; and as it became less and less necessary to prove the truth of Christianity by external signs, and powers, and miracles. Physical miracles were useless, after the Church had been firmly established; for the Church itself, when established, was a standing miracle, and embraced "manifold wonders in its bosom".

The working of the spiritual-religious power of Christianity is its greatest miracle; and it is a miracle that will continue to operate as long as the Church shall exist. Hence, the outward, physical miracle is called, in the New Testament, "*a sign*", "*a power*"; a *sign* of a higher order of life, a *power* proceeding from the invisible world. The miracle-working power of the early Church has long since passed away; but the Church itself still stands, a perpetual miracle of God's providence and love. "How meanly", then, it has been well said by Prof. Trench, "do we esteem of a

Church, of its marvellous gifts, of the powers of the coming world which are working within it, of its Word, of its Sacraments, when it seems to us a small thing that in it men are new-born, raised from the death of sin to the life of righteousness, the eyes of their understanding enlightened, and their ears opened; unless we can also tell of more visible and sensuous wonders. It is as though the heavens should not declare to us the glory of God, nor the firmament shew us his handiwork, except at some single moment, such as that when the sun was standing still upon Gibeon, and the moon in Ajalon."[15]

The miracle-working power was necessary in the early history of Christianity; for then the new faith had to contend against adverse and opposing influences, the force of which we, at this day, can hardly estimate. When the Church no longer needed such confirmation of her divine mission, "when to the wisdom of God it appeared that He had adequately confirmed the Word with signs following", the power of performing miracles ceased to be granted; and the Church, now firmly established in the world, was left to be itself a standing miracle for all coming time.

Beautifully and truthfully has Prof. Hagenbach expressed himself on this point, in his admirable popular History of the Early Christian Church:[16]—"That from a corner of Judea, that from one who was crucified, and from the community of his disciples chosen from the lowest classes of mankind, there went forth a power which proclaimed destruction to the great Roman Empire, and prepared it inwardly before it had been made ready by external circumstances; that neither fire and sword, nor all the wisdom and eloquence of the world, that neither falsehood and calumny, nor the alluring prospect of rest and ease, could restrain those who believed from bearing witness to what they had experienced from without and within; that a blazing spark was cast into a world of sin and error, and that this spark kindled a fire which no might and no art of men could put out; that the most hardened and the most corrupt hearts were seized and wrought upon by the power of a truth which gave them no rest until they had found peace with God; that the lowliest and the

---

15   Notes on the Miracles of our Lord, N. Y. edit., p. 51.

16   Die Christliche Kirche der drei ersten Jahrhunderte, pp. 344, 345. This work of Hagenbach fs is an admirable popular Compend of the Church History of the First Three Centuries. Rev. T. W. Tobey, of North Carolina, thinks of putting it in an English dress; doing which, he would perform a useful and creditable labor.

despised among the people learned to feel themselves a kingly race, called to rule the world and to judge the world;—all this is a great miracle, a wondrous fact which can not be denied, which cannot be explained by mechanical and outward influences; but can be comprehended only by admitting the principle which gave it its impulse and power; and this principle is none other than the unlimited principle of the eternal love and mercy of God. God wills that all men shall receive help; that all shall come to the knowledge of the truth, and that all shall attain to peace and to eternal life. This is the everlasting law of the divine government of the universe; a law which perfects itself in the history of the Church, in its struggle with the world and its unfriendly powers, but in a struggle carried on in confident expectation of future victory, even perfection in glory".

§3. THE ETHICS, OR MORAL DOCTRINES OF THE EARLY CHURCH.

No System of Morals, as such, taught in the New Testament—Christianity a Life, not an Ethical System—Christian Life liable to Extremes—The Morality of the Early Church, the Morality of Reason—A Higher Life proceeding from God, and bringing forth "The Fruits of the Spirit".

The teachings of Jesus, and subsequently of the Apostles, did not shape themselves into a fixed and positive system. They taught, indeed, the highest truths; but taught them as occasion demanded, and not in a definite and unalterable form. The Gospels and the Epistles of the New Testament, embody the life-imparting truths of Christianity; but they do not present them in a systematic arrangement. Christianity was *a life,* not *a system;* a life implanted in the soul from heaven, and controlled by the Spirit of God. The truths on which the soul was to be nurtured, were communicated first by Christ, and after his departure by the Spirit, "to the Church of the living God", to act in it and through it to the end of the world. The guardians of the Church were first the Apostles, and then the apostolic and other inspired writings of the New Testament. These were, and are, the divinely-appointed interpreters of Christian truth, as long as the Church shall exist. This truth, however, is not stated for us in a strictly scientific form. The New Testament knows no system of doctrine, no system of morals, *as such.* Yet it is all doctrine and all morals; revealed for the government and guidance of believers in every age.

The New Testament represents Christianity as an active principle, a new life, in him that comes to Jesus as the Son of God. Its morality is a morality not so much based on positive law, as springing from the internal promptings of the Holy Spirit. If contrasted with the stern legality of Judaism, or with the rigid stoicism of some systems of ancient heathen Philosophy, Christianity appears, as to the morals which it inculcates, as an unfettered activity of the new-born man, proceeding not from the law of ordinances, but from the law of faith and love. Contrasted, however, with the freedom of Epicurean heathenism, it appears as a law of strict restraint; confined to narrow limits by the stern and unyielding discipline of the Spirit.

Christian life is liable to develop itself into opposite extremes; that of a too soulless conformity to outward precepts, and that of a too unlimited freedom from the wholesome restraints of the Spirit of faith and love. It did so in early times. A rigorous mode of life, well called Montanism, exhibited itself, sometimes, in those whose mental constitution and habits inclined them to bind themselves by the fixed and known restraints of a religion, of precepts and ordinances; while a freedom unallowed by the Spirit, well styled Gnosticism, was apt to be manifested in those whose minds led them to a life of contemplation rather than a life of activity in the work of the Lord. But these opposite tendencies both overleaped the bounds of genuine Christianity; and it was one office of the early Church, through the Apostles, and its other distinguished teachers, to keep back its sons from either extreme, and to restrain them, by bonds of love, within the limits of Christian prudence and moderation.

The Church did this; not, however, by finding and occupying a mean **between** these two extremes; but by taking a surer and better position **above** them both. It strove to lead its membership to struggle through from the law of the letter to the law of freedom; to reach that height to which Paul had attained, when he said, "All things are lawful unto me, but all things are not expedient."

The Christianity of the early Church, unlike all other positive systems of religion, gave no purely outward and arbitrary moral commands; such as were not grounded in the moral nature of man, and such as looked only to the regulation of the external relations of life. In a certain sense, one may say that its morality is none other than the morality which is recognized by the eternal laws of human reason. And yet, working by means of this pure, reason-recognized morality, which it displays in all its elements, Christianity reaches beyond the capacity of the natural man, and beyond his views, his expectations, and his powers. It makes him a holy, and yet a joyous, being; bold and resolute, yet mild, forgiving, and patient. It demands watchfulness without excitement; temperance without a rigid self-denial in meats and drinks, and in the enjoyments of life; soberness without sadness; a constant looking to the heavenly and the eternal, without neglecting the secular business of life, in which, on the contrary, it rather requires a faithfulness which shall overlook no duty, even the smallest and the least important. The morality of Christianity is, we may say then, a supernatural and yet an entirely natural, a superhuman and yet an altogether human, morality: it transcends the powers of the rational man, not only by what it demands, but by what it gives,—what it creates in him by the Holy Spirit which is shed forth into the hearts of believers. Hence the Apostle Paul says nothing of a new Law, but speaks of a "*fruit of the Spirit*", which "is love, joy, peace, long-suffering, gentleness, goodness, faith, meekness, temperance".

§4. THE PUBLIC AND PRIVATE LIFE OF THE ANCIENT BAPTISTS.

Early Christians, Models of Piety—Called to a "Holy Warfare for God and Christ"—Kept aloof from the Amusements of Heathenism—Suffered Death, rather than recognize Paganism, and reject Christ—Yet, Lived among and for the Heathen—Christian Wives with Pagan Husbands—Baptist Lady "of the Olden Time"—Slaves, honored in the Church, and instruments of Converting the Heathen—Brotherly Love, distinguishing Trait of the Primitive Baptists—Observed by the Unbelieving—Warmest in Times of Persecution—Not Confined to the Church at Home—Brethren differing in Opinion, differed in Love—Love of the Early Christians towards the Heathen—Preached to them, and Acted before them, "Christ Crucified".

Christians of the Baptist Church of the first three centuries exemplified in their lives the distinctive traits of the Gospel. Their minds were wholly devoted to Christ and to his service. They carried their religion with them into all the relations of life. Christianity with them was not a mere profession: it was an active existence, a living, breathing, reality. Separate from the world, they yet lived in the world, to bring men by their example to Christ; "the salt of the earth," shining forth as lights among a wicked and benighted people. Living lives of simplicity and truthfulness; strong in the faith of the Gospel, and in Christian purity and holiness; filled with love to God, to the brotherhood, and to all mankind,—these Baptists of the early Church were models of piety and zeal in the work of the Lord.

The Baptist of this age of the Church felt bound to live up to the vow of obedience to Jesus (his **sacramentum,** or **oath**) which he took on receiving the ordinance of baptism; when he solemnly engaged to renounce Satan and all his works; and declared, by a symbolic action of beautiful significancy, that he had "put off the old man with his deeds", and that, being buried with Christ, he would rise with Him to walk in righteousness and holiness forever. Created anew unto good works in Christ Jesus, he viewed his calling "as a holy warfare for God and Christ against all the powers of darkness", and against all that should oppose itself to the reign of Jesus in the hearts of men. Hence, though he was obedient to the laws of the government under which he lived, he could take no part in any thing which seemed to recognize the truth of heathenism. He kept himself aloof from all its idolatrous worship and ceremonies. Its festivals, its triumphal marches, its gladiatorial shows, and its theatrical exhibitions, he carefully avoided. Even its musical concerts, and its exhibitions of art, he was loathe to attend; for they were each interpenetrated with the leaven of idolatry.

Bather than violate the honest scruples of his conscience, he would suffer death. And many Christians were led to execution, in this period of the history of the Church, by the enraged and misguided heathen. They died in triumph. Few wavered: few yielded, when called upon to deny Christ. They endured to the end; feeling as did Polycarp, who, about to be led to the stake, in his old age, said, in words of touching tenderness, "Eighty and six years have I served him [Christ], and he has done me nothing but good: how then can I speak reproachfully of him, my Lord and my Saviour?" They despised the pleasures of earth; and wanted only the joy which comes from God, the "joy unspeakable and full of glory". Their pleasures were high and holy; "the contempt of every thing earthly, true liberty, a clear conscience, and a contented life, free from the fear of death".

Christianity was compelled, however, to come frequently into contact with heathenism. It could do so lawfully, so long as it did not recognize idolatry as a true religion. Nay, the believer was even bound, in some respects, to seek the heathen; for it was his duty to convert them to the truth. It was necessary, therefore, to obtain their friendship and good will. He might mingle with them freely in private life; being careful to "keep himself unspotted from the world".

A believer married to an unbeliever, broke not the marriage tie, when converted to Christ; but sought, by and through it, to bring the other to the same life-imparting reception of the Gospel. The Christian wife was thus made an instrument for the conversion of her husband; and, through her means, often, their children, instructed in the Gospel, were brought to a saving knowledge of the Redeemer.—So, the pious Monica sowed in the mind of the young Augustine, the seeds which were afterwards to spring up, and bring forth fruit abundantly to the honor and glory of God. So, too, the godly Nonna, who converted her husband from paganism, like Hannah, the mother of Samuel, devoted her son, Gregory Nazianzen, to God, before he was born; and, immediately after his birth (about 325 A. D.), carried him to the altar, and, laying a book of the Gospels under his hand, consecrated him to the service of his Saviour. His early consecration gave tone and character to the whole of Gregory's subsequent life.

The Christian woman not only brought up her children "in the nurture and admonition of the Lord", and set to her family an example of faith and patience; but she also performed offices of charity and love to the brethren at large. "She seeks not", says Tertullian (*De Cult. Fem.* c. 10), "the heathen theatres; but she goes forth to search for brethren who are ill, to partake of the communion, and to hear the word of God. Her chief occupation is, to seek out those who are imprisoned for conscience sake, to visit the sick brethren even in the poorest huts, and to receive into her house and entertain traveling brethren from abroad". Such was the Baptist lady of the olden time.

Every believer, of whatever station, had his appropriate work in the early Church. Slaves, as well as freemen,—many of whom were called into "the glorious liberty of the Gospel,—labored to spread the good news of salvation. They stood high in the Church, in which there was neither bond nor free, but all were one in Christ Jesus. Through their influence, not a few from among the heathen were brought from darkness into light. In pagan families, where they often had the oversight of the children, they sowed in the minds of the young the seeds of Christian instruction; and, not unfrequently, they did not point to Christ in vain. The truth lodged in the hearts of the children, often ripened, at a later day, into perfect knowledge that made wise unto salvation.

Perhaps, the most distinguishing trait of the early Christian Baptists was their love for the brethren. Their mutual affection was such as to astonish the heathen; who used to exclaim in wonder, "See how these Christians love one another!" To the malicious scoffer, this brotherly union appeared ridiculous; and he would ironically say, with the mocker Lucian, "Your law-giver has persuaded you that ye are all brethren." In the jealous world, this affection excited suspicion; "for the Christians", they said, "know one another by secret signs; and love one another almost before they are acquainted". What a testimony in favor of that religion which professes to be the perfection of love to God and love to man!

Especially did this fraternal affection manifest itself in times of persecution. A church would appropriate its funds to supply the wants of its imprisoned members; and individual believers in it would vie with one another in ministering to the necessities of the captives. Their spiritual, as well as their temporal, wants were fully supplied; and "ministers were sent into the prisons, to read and explain the Word of God to the confessors who had been weakened by tortures".

This brotherly love was not confined to members of the same church: it extended itself to all Christians. Any believer, on coming to a strange city, would meet with a warm reception from the brethren, if he could show a testimonial from the pastor of the church with which he was connected. If he desired to remain and engage in business, the brethren would look him out some suitable occupation.

One church, too, would aid another; the richer contributing to the necessities of the poorer in this world's goods. On one occasion, in Cyprian's time, the church in Carthage, North Africa, sent a large sum (more than four thousand dollars) to certain churches of Numidia, to aid in ransoming some of their members from captivity.

When brother differed in opinion from brother, he strove to do it in love. In combating what they thought to be error, the saints, as was meet, proceeded in the spirit of gentleness and patience. If repelled, they answered not "with hate and persecution, but with the manifestation of peace and true love". "We gain much", says Chrysostom, "showing love and the true spirit of a disciple of Christ. We must condemn false doctrines; but in every way spare the men who espouse them, and pray for their salvation." Such was the love Baptists entertained for each other in the times of early Christianity. It was holy, pure, sincere, and abiding. Love they each other so to-day? An affection of this kind is god-like; and forms a bond of union between brethren that is stronger than a chain of adamant.

The Baptists at this time not only loved one another: they loved all men, and sought to do good unto all. They aided the heathen, as well as the brethren, in their earthly troubles, by means of earthly consolations. An example of this world-embracing benevolence was given by Cyprian's church, during the great plague in Carthage. Numbers of the dead and dying being cast forth by their pagan friends to lie unburied in the highways, the brethren, rich and poor, stimulated by their loved bishop, "furnished money and help to bury the bodies of their persecutors, and to rescue the city from the danger of a more terrible devastation".

The surest proof, however, which these Christians gave of their love to the heathen, was their earnest striving, by precept and example, to bring them to Christ. Not the clergy only, but all believers, took a part, each in his own sphere, in advancing the interests of the religion of Christ. Each one had his own work to do; and each did it. Each preached the Gospel, if not by word, yet in his life. In the age of the Apostles, and that immediately succeeding, every believer was a preacher of the truth as it is in Jesus; though each was not a teacher in the Church.—Every man and every woman took some active part of spreading a knowledge of Christianity, Every believer tried to bring others to Christ. He that was a true Christian, so far from finding it impossible to win others,—found it impossible *not* to do it: his love to the Redeemer *would* speak forth, and would be heard. So labor, in our day, the Baptists in Germany,—fit descendants of the Baptists of Apostolic times. This is "aggressive Christianity" in the only sense in which Christianity may be aggressive; and thus attacking, it must conquer the world.

§5. THE "LIFE IN CHRIST" OF THE PRIMITIVE BAPTISTS.

Primitive Believers "lived unto God"—Justin Martyr's Description of Baptist Life in the Beginning of the Second Century—Church Vitalized by the Spirit—Portraiture of Christian Life about 132 A. D., by the Author of the Epistle to Diognetus—Christianity thus Active and Vigorous, Operative in the World—The Bounds of the Church Extensive even at the Close of the First Century—The Conduct of the Primitive Baptists, a Model for the Baptists of All Ages—Propagated as in Apostolic and Early Days, Baptist Truth will Spread to the Confines of the World.

Thus have we briefly glanced at the morals and the private life of the Baptists of the Early Church. Christianity in this age was a life. Having given themselves to Christ, believers lived, henceforth, not unto themselves but unto God. Regenerated by the Spirit, they followed the leading of the Spirit; and the Church of God increased and multiplied. Justin Martyr thus describes the Baptists of his day; and he flourished in the first half of the second century:—"We, who were once slaves of lust, now have our chief joy in a pious life. Once, we loved gain above every thing else; now, we give our possessions for the common good, and distribute to every one that is needy. Once, we hated and murdered one another; we would not receive into our houses people of foreign climes, because they had different customs from our own. Now, since the appearance of Christ, we permit them to be our guests. We pray for our enemies. We strive to convince those who hate us unjustly; so that, living according to the glorious teaching of Christ, they may obtain the joyful hope of a participation in the blessings which are prepared for us by God Almighty. Christ commanded us to use no violence, and not to return evil for evil. He exhorted us, by our patience and gentleness, to convert all men. In many among us, we can show you that this has actually been done They have been changed from violent and tyrannical men, and subdued; while they have either observed the steadfast endurance of Christian neighbors, or have become acquainted with the extraordinary patience of Christian travelers, suffering injustice, or have seen the conduct of the Christian under various circumstances, in the intercourse of life."[17]

So wonderful a change as this, produced in men who had once been the slaves of their corrupt passions and lusts, could have been brought about only by the transforming and renewing Spirit of God. The Church was yet young and vigorous; and though neither perfect in doctrine, nor spotless in conduct, it was full of life, and health, and beauty. She was "as a bride adorned for her husband". She "had all the freshness, enthusiasm, and vigor of a youthful giant, inspired by the breath of God"; and she went forth as an army with banners, "conquering and to conquer". The life of the Spirit made her "vital in every part", and "the fruit of the Spirit" was love, and peace, and joy. An unknown Author,—once thought, but erroneously, to be Justin Martyr,—who wrote about 132 A.D., the following highly interesting and life-like description of the Christian Baptists of his time; and shows what kind of fruit the

---

17   Quoted in the Christian Review, March, 1848, p. 52.

young and vigorous tree of the Church was wont, in his day, to produce "for the healing of the nations":

"The Christians are kept distinct from the rest of men, neither by their dwellings, nor by their language and customs. Although they reside in the cities of the Greeks and barbarians, according as his lot has fallen to each, and, in respect to their raiment and food, as well as other things pertaining to this earthly existence, follow the customary habits of the land, yet they are distinguished by a wonderful and universally remarkable manner of life. They dwell in their own father-land, but as strangers; they take part in all as citizens, yet endure all as foreigners. Every country, however strange, is to them a home; and every home is to them a foreign land. They marry, as do others, and have families. But they do not expose their children, as the heathen do. They live *in* the flesh, but not *after* the flesh. They dwell upon the earth, but they live in heaven; they obey the established laws, and by their life raise themselves above the land. They love all; and are persecuted by all, rejected, and condemned. They are slain, and made alive. They are poor, and make all rich. They have want in all and abundance in all. They are insulted and bless.

"In a word, what the soul is in the body, that Christians are in the world. As the soul is spread throughout all the members of the body, so are Christians spread in all the cities of the world. The soul indeed dwells in the body, but it is not of the body. So Christians dwell *in* the world, but are not *of* the world. The invisible soul is enclosed in a visible body. So men know Christians as inhabitants of the world, but their worship of God remains an invisible worship. The flesh hates and contends with the soul; but the soul does no harm to the flesh, but rather hinders it from giving way to its appetites. So the world hates Christians; although they do men of the world no harm, but, on the contrary, oppose their evil desires and lusts. The soul loves the flesh which hates it; the Christians love those by whom they are hated. The soul is shut up in the body; and this it is which holds the body together. So Christians in the world are kept under guard; and yet it is they who hold the world together, and save it from being dissolved. The immortal soul dwells in the mortal body; and Christians dwell as foreigners in this perishable life, expecting an imperishable existence in heaven. An office of such importance has God given them in the world, and this they can never forget."

How touching a description is this of the life of the first Baptists! How simple, yet how grand, is it in its wondrous beauty! It is not strange, that superstition and idolatry fell before the onslaught of a Church so knit together in love, and so animated by the Spirit of the living God. Men and women were transformed as by magic into ardent and self-sacrificing believers in Jesus. The synagogues of the Jews were converted into Christian churches; and the temples of idolatry into the temples of God. Christianity, pure, unadulterated, primitive Baptist Christianity, spread like wild-fire throughout the world. "There is not a nation", says Justin Martyr, "whether Greek or barbarian,, or of any other name, even of those who wander in tribes, or live in tents, among whom prayers and thanksgivings are not offered to the Father and Creator of the universe, in the name of the crucified Jesus" Unlike every system of ancient Philosophy, Christianity was not the religion of a few, but a religion for all mankind; and, being such, its doctrines, adapted as they are to all men everywhere, spread at once throughout the whole world, into every nation, and village, and city; "converting both whole houses and separate individuals", and bringing all men,—learned, and unlearned, the untutored slave, and the proudest philosopher,—by the power of God, unto salvation.

The brotherly love of these primitive Baptists, their benevolence towards each other and towards the world, their calm and patient endurance of the hostility of unbelievers, and their heart-felt and active zeal for Christianity, make them models for imitation in the Church as long as the foundation of the earth shall stand. Christian professors were not, even in that day, perfect in righteousness; but they reached a height in holiness which few believers since have been able to attain. Bound together by a common love to Christ, and having one aim and one hope in life, they were of one heart, and of one mind, and of one soul. "They left all to follow Christ. They lived a spiritual, self-denying and happy life. Full of love to Christ, and to one another, they constituted a family, bound together by holy ties, rejoicing in common privileges and common aims. Their purity, their simplicity, their affection, their courage, their joy, struck the heathen, astonished the world. They bore all sufferings for Christ's sake, not only with patience, but with serenity. Not even death, bloody and cruel, could separate them from the love of Christ. They lived, they died, for immortality. Hence it is not surprising that, thirty years after the death of Christ, the triumphs of the cross had extended not only over Palestine, but to almost every part of Asia the less, the isles of the Ægean sea, a large-portion of

Greece, and even as far as Rome. At the close of the first century, or seventy years from the crucifixion of Christ, Christianity had penetrated into every part of the Roman Empire. It was planted in Rome and in Carthage, in Athens and Alexandria, in Ephesus and Antioch, in Damascus and Babylon; nay more, it had reached, if we may believe the traditions of the Church, as far as Spain on the one hand, and India on the other. Christians were to be numbered by hundreds and thousands in Palestine and Greece, in Italy and Egypt, in Ethiopia and in Asia Minor."[18]

This was the Christianity of the Apostolic and Early Baptist Church. Do we find it in our day? Give us this, and we shall soon bring all men to the knowledge of Jesus; whom to know is life eternal. Let Baptists preserve the simplicity which has long distinguished them; let them hold on unwavering to the religion of the Early Church and of the New Testament; let them keep alive their warm enthusiasm in the cause of Christ, feeding it, as in ancient times, with the oil of purity and love; let them be earnest yet cautious, impetuous yet calm, aggressive yet peaceful, grasping in one hand the shield of faith, and waving in the other "the sword of the Spirit, which is the Word of God",—and they will themselves be built up in the most holy faith, and will be blessed in their efforts to establish a pure Gospel Christianity in every kingdom and government of the earth.

Let Baptists in America, and in England, and everywhere, imitate the zeal of the Early Church. They have the truth on their side; let them use it wisely, and all will be well. Let their efforts as private Christians be redoubled, and be put forth with the sincerity and energy of the primitive believers; let their Pulpit-Preaching be animated by the Spirit which burned in Peter; let their Religious Press exhibit the vital power and the love of the truth which are shown in the Epistles of Paul; and they shall come off conquerors, and more than conquerors, over every form of opposition from without and from within, and over all that is inimical to the purity and simplicity of the Gospel. "If", to use the words of another, "they can be at peace among themselves; be of one mind, waste no strength in internal disputes; unite in building up and perfecting their own institutions, rather than pulling down those of their neighbors; promote unity, system, peace, brotherly-love, and the love of learning and active usefulness among their ministry and members;—if they *can* and *will* do these things, the Baptists have a glorious future"; this is the true policy

18   Rev. Dr. Turnbull, in Christian Review, Sept. 1844, p. 342.

for Baptists; let them adopt it, and they will certainly flourish. Let them renounce the spirit of the world, and be wholly clothed upon with the spirit of Christ. Let them write, as their motto, "Peace on earth and good will to men", on their banners of love; then let them move on to the peaceful conquest of the world. Let Baptists do these things, and their progress will be onward and upward "to the perfect day".

CHAPTER FIFTH: SUPPLEMENTARY.
FURTHER AND SURE PROOFS THAT THE APOSTOLIC AND THE EARLY CHURCH PRACTISED ONLY BELIEVER'S IMMERSION.

§1. PÆDO-BAPTIST ADMISSIONS IN FAVOR OF IMMERSION,

Modern pædo-baptist Admissions—Concessions of Rev. Dr. Schaff—Admissions of Conybeare and Howson—Roman Catholics defend Pouring and Sprinkling by Tradition—Testimony of Rt. Rev. Dr. Trevern—The Greek Church against the Roman Catholic Tradition—Testimony of the Greek Book *"To Pedalion"*—Concessions of Rev. Prof. Stuart—Admissions of Rev. Dr. Coleman—Rev. Dr. Chalmers on Rom. 6: 3–7?Admissions of Rev. Dr. Geo. Campbell, and Rev. Dr. S. T. Bloomfield—Rosenmlüler's Testimony—Regrets of Jeremy Taylor, Dr. Whitby, and Bishop Smith—Testimony of Dr. Charles Anthon, arid Mr. Geo. Wyndham—Liddell and Scott's Lexicon, and Prof. Drisler—Testimony of Distinguished German Biblical Critics: Neander, Tholuck, Olshausen, Knapp, Storr and Flatt, and Hagenbach—Still other German Concessions: from Starke, Bretschneider, Schleusner, Wahl, Lange, Scholz, Rheinhard, Paulus, Fritsche, Augusti, Von Cölln, Gieseler, Guericke, Von Meyer, Starck, Hahn, Winer, and Mosheim—The Position Established.

The truth of the Baptist position that immersion alone was considered baptism in Apostolic times, may be established from the admissions of pædo-baptists themselves. A volume might be made out of these concessions. Many, especially those of the more ancient pædo-baptist divines, maybe found in a convenient form in Rev. A. Booth's "Pædo-baptism Examined". It is our purpose to add here a few of the more modern admissions, especially those of the most eminent biblical critics of Germany. We need not think of attempting to cite all; for so unanimous is the sentiment of well-read theologians of every denomination, on this point, that it would be difficult to find any scholar of acknowledged reputation, who entertains on this subject any other than the belief that, during the life-time of the Apostles, and for a considerable period afterwards, immersion alone was practised as baptism by the Church.

The first concession we shall adduce is that of the Rev. Dr. Philip Schaff, Prof, in the Lutheran Theological Seminary at Mercersburg, Penn. He is a German by birth and education, but has been residing some years in America. The extracts here given are taken from a learned and valuable work, lately published, entitled "History of the Apostolic Church". This testimony is the more useful because Prof. S is an opponent of the views and practices of the Baptists, and considers them "a hyper-spiritualistic sect". He admits that the Baptists are right "as to the form of baptism", and yet strangely enough he thinks they "go too far," when, "in Judaic legal letter service, they declare immersion the only valid form of baptism". The first quotation is from p. 568, of the History:

Immersion, and not sprinkling, was unquestionably the original, normal form (i. e. of baptism). This is shown by the very meaning of the Greek words *baptizo, baptisma, baptismos,* used to designate the rite. Then again, by the analogy of the baptism of John, which was performed in the Jordan (*en,* Matt. 3: 6, compare 16; also *eis ton Iordanen,* Mk. 1, 9). Furthermore, by the New Testament comparisons of baptism with the passage through the Red Sea (1 Cor. 10: 2), with the flood (1 Pet. 3: 21), with a bath (Eph. 5. 26; Tit. 3: 5), with a burial and resurrection (Rom. 6: 4; Col. 2: 12). Finally, by the general usage of ecclesiastical antiquity, which was always immersion (as it is to this day in the Oriental and also the Graeco-Russian churches); pouring and sprinkling being substituted only in cases of urgent necessity, such as sickness and approaching death."

These are the leading arguments used by the Baptists. They are here summed up briefly. Dr. S., it will be observed, speaks of the "*analogy* of the baptism of John"; which shows that he considers the rite administered by John *not* identical in significance with Christian baptism. It can not be said that he takes this view *because* he is a Pædo-baptist; for he admits, in the same breath, that the Baptists are right in their position respecting the Act of Baptism. The same remark may be made of *all* those German Pædo-baptist critics (and they are many) who, while frankly surrendering to us our positions respecting the Act and Subjects of Baptism, do not think Johns's baptism identical with the Christian ordinance.

Two pages in advance, Dr Schaff reiterates in a Note, his testimony; mentioning, at the same time, other Pædo-baptist authorities who have testified to the same effect. The quotation credited to Conybeare and Howson, is from a work of theirs entitled "The Life and Epistles of St. Paul," published in England in 1852. They are both English scholars of reputation:

"The ordinary use of ***baptizein, baptisma, baptismos,*** in connection with the passages respecting baptism adduced in the text, the clear testimonies of antiquity, and the present prevailing usage of the Oriental churches, puts it beyond all doubt, that entire or partial immersion was the general rule of Christian antiquity, from which certainly nothing but urgent outward circumstances caused a deviation. Respecting the form of baptism, therefore (quite otherwise with the much more important difference respecting the subjects of baptism or infant baptism), ***the impartial historian is compelled by exegesis and history substantially to yield the point to the Baptists,*** as is done in fact (perhaps somewhat too decidedly and without due regard to the arguments just stated for the other practice) by most German scholars, e. g. Neander, Apostelgesch. I. p. 276; Knapp, Vorlesungen über die christliche Glaubenslehre, II., p. 453; Höfling, 1. c. I. p. 47 sqq.; also by the Anglican divines, Conybeare and Howson, Life of St. Paul, I. 471: 'It is needless to add that baptism was (unless in exceptional cases) administered by immersion, the convert being plunged beneath the surface of the water, to represent his death to the life of sin; and then raised from this momentary burial to represent his resurrection to the life of righteousness. It must be a subject of regret that the general discontinuance of this original form of baptism (though perhaps necessary in our northern climates) has rendered obscure to popular apprehension some very important passages of Scripture.'—With this we entirely concur. It is well known that the Reformers, Luther and Calvin, and several old Protestant liturgies, gave the preference to immersion; and this is undoubtedly far better suited than sprinkling to symbolize the idea of baptism, the entire purifying of the inward man, the being buried and rising again with Christ."

The Roman Catholics defend their practice of sprinkling on the ground of tradition; admitting frankly that baptism in the most ancient times was immersion.

They charge Pædo-baptist Protestants with inconsistency, when they contend that every article of Christian faith and practise is contained in the New Testament, and yet, without support from Scripture, practise sprinkling and pouring. The Right Rev. Dr, Trevern, a high dignitary of the Roman Church, wrote, in 1847, a book called "La Discussion Amicale", and addressed it to the Protestant Clergy, especially of England. Its object is to show up Protestant inconsistencies. Touching Sprinkling, or Pouring, he has the following in his second volume (p. 142):

"But, without going any farther, show us, my Lords, the validity of your baptism, 'by ***Scripture alone***'. Jesus Christ there ordains that it shall be conferred, not by pouring water on the heads of believers, but by believers being plunged into water. The word ***baptizo,*** employed by the Evangelists, strictly conveys this signification, as the learned are agreed; and, at the head of them, Casaubon, of all the Caivinists, the best versed in the Greek language. Now, baptism by immersion has ceased for many ages, and you yourselves, as well as we, have only received it by infusion. It would, therefore, be all over with your baptism, unless you established it by tradition and the practice of the Church. This being settled, I ask you, from whom have you received baptism? Is it not from the church of Rome? And what do you think of her? Do you not consider her as heretical, and even idolatrous? You cannot, then, according to the terms of Scripture, prove the validity of your baptism; and to produce a plea for it, you are obliged to seek it with Pope Stephen and the councils of Arles and Nice, and in Apostolic tradition.

Next in order to this testimony of a Roman Catholic against pædo-baptist Protestants, it may not be amiss to quote the testimony of the Greek Church against the Catholics, on account of their "traditional" sprinkling. The "Pedalion", a folio of 484 pages, the standard work of the Greek Church for its Faith, Practice, and Government,—a work "duly authenticated by the Patriarch and holy Synod",—contains a long article under the 46th and 47th canons, showing the falsity of baptism in the Roman Church; an article which "the author thinks very important at the present time, on account of the differences not only between the Greek Church and the Roman Catholic, but also between it and all others who, like the Catholic, practise sprinkling." For the extracts given below and the accompanying remarks, we are indebted to a translation of the Rev. Mr. Love, of Mass., who rendered from the original.

"We say that the baptism of the Latins", (Roman Catholics) is "***baptism falsely named***", (***pseudonumon baptisma***). * * * Again, "The Latins are heretics of old, specially from the very fact that they are UN-***baptized***", (***abaptistoi***). * * * Again, "The more ancient Latins, the first to make innovations upon apostolic baptism, practised pouring, (***epichusin***) that is, they poured a little water upon the crown of the child's head. And this is still practised in some places at the present time. More, however, now, with a bunch of hogs' bristles throw a few drops of water thrice upon the child's forehead."

Again, "Observe that we do not say, that we ***re-baptize*** (***anabaptizomen***); the Latins, but that we BAPTIZE (***baptizomen***) them, since their baptism (***baptisma***) is a lie in its very name", ***pseudetai to onoma auto.*** "It is not ***baptism*** at all, (***kai oukolos esti baptisma,***) but bare sprinkling", (***rantisma***).

Such are a few of the very many extracts which I might make from this book of the highest authority in the Greek Church,—a book which nowhere mentions ***sprinkling*** for ***baptism,*** but which utterly forbids it, and by the authority of the Greek Church anathematizes all who practise it. Thus again under "Canon 50, apostolical", the author having made immersion and emersion, (***going under*** the water and ***rising out*** of it) necessary to ***baptism,*** adds, "Not only does ***baptism*** not consist without these, but neither without them could it be ***called baptism***", and gives for his reason that the act of baptizing is called baptism from the ***immersion in the water and not from any other thing.***

The late Moses Stuart, Prof, in the Theological Seminary at Andover Mass.,—one of the best biblical scholars whom America has produced—bears testimony in favor of the Baptist view:

In his book on the "Mode of Baptism," a work of equal candor and scholarship, he makes the following admissions: "***Bapto*** and ***Baptizo*** mean ***to dip, plunge,*** or ***immerge,*** into any thing liquid. All lexicographers and critics of any note are agreed in this" (p. 14). He says in another place, "From the earliest ages of which we have any account, subsequent to the apostolic age, and downward for several centuries, the churches did generally practice baptism by immersion; perhaps by immersion of the whole person; and the only exceptions to this mode which were usually allowed, were in cases of urgent sickness, or other cases of immediate and imminent danger, where immersion could not be practised." In an article in the Bib. Repository (vol. 3, p. 359), the same theologian remarks: " 'It is,' says Augusti, 'a thing made out,' viz., the ancient practice of immersion. So indeed all the writers who have thoroughly investigated the subject. I know of no one usage of ancient times which seems to be more clearly made out. I can not see how it is possible for any candid man who examines the subject to deny this."

The Rev. L. Coleman, a Pædo-baptist scholar of considerable distinction as a writer, gives his testimony in favor of the Baptist position; though by no means a favorer of Baptist doctrines, and an opponent of the sentiment that immersion is essential to baptism. In his work entitled "Ancient Christianity Exemplified", he has the following:

"In the primitive church, immediately subsequent to the age of the apostles this (immersion) was undeniably the common mode of baptism. The utmost that can be said of *sprinkling* in that early period is that it was, in case of necessity, permitted as an exception to a general rule. . . . . . It is a great mistake to suppose that baptism by immersion was discontinued when infant baptism became generally prevalent; the practise of immersion continued even until the thirteenth or fourteenth century" (p. 395).

The late Rev. Dr. Chalmers, a distinguished Presbyterian clergyman of Scotland, testifies thus to the original meaning of baptism in his Lectures on Romans, while commenting on chapter 6: 3–7:

"The original meaning of the word baptism is immersion; and though we regard it as a point of indifference whether the ordinance so named be performed in this way or by sprinkling, yet we doubt not that the prevalent style of the administration in the apostles' days was of an actual submerging of the whole body under water."

Dr. George Campbell, another distinguished Scotch Presbyterian,—a better scholar even than Dr. Chalmers,—testifies to the same effect. He says, very justly, that the meaning of *baptizo* both in sacred authors, and in classical, is "***to dip, to plunge, to immerse***; and declares that, in the Fathers, "it is always construed suitably to this meaning".

Rev. Dr. Bloomfield,—well known in this country by his Commentary on the New Testament,—makes the following remarks on Rom. 6: 4., in his "Critical Digest":

"There is here plainly a reference to the ancient mode of baptism by immersion; and I agree with Koppe and Rosenmüller (two German commentators), that there is reason to regret it should have been abandoned in most Christian churches, especially as it has so evidently a reference to the mystic sense of baptism."

Rosenmüller, *a*s here referred to, says: "Immersion in the water of baptism, a coming forth out of it, was a symbol of a person's renouncing his former life, and, on the contrary, beginning a new one. The learned have rightly reminded us that, on account of this emblematical meaning of baptism, the rite of immersion ought to have been retained in the Christian Church."

Not a few clergymen of the Episcopal Church, have, like Bloomfield, regretted the departure from the original practice of immersion. The learned and eloquent Bishop Jeremy Taylor († 1667), like John Wesley of a later day, condemned "the practice of sprinkling altogether, as contrary both to the analogy of the ceremony, the Apostolic tradition, and the canons of the English and Irish Church." So says his biographer, Bishop Heber. The pious Dr. ***Daniel Whitby,*** († 1726),—often quoted by Bloomfield in his New Testament,—speaks warmly on this point, when commenting, in his N. T. Commentary, on Rom. 6: 4: "It being so expressly declared here and Col. 2: 12, that we are 'buried with Christ in baptism,' by being buried under water, and the argument to oblige us to a conformity to his death, by dying to sin, being taken thence; and this immersion being religiously observed by ***all Christians for thirteen centuries,*** and approved by our church, and the change of it into sprinkling, even without any allowance from the author of this institution, or any license from any council of the Church, being that Which the Romanist still urges to justify his refusal of the cup to the laity; it were to be wished that this custom might be again of general use, and aspersion only permitted, as of old, in case of the Clinic, or in present danger of death." ***Bishop Smith,*** of Kentucky, expressed a like desire some years ago, wishing that immersion might be restored among the Episcopalians; and even going so far as to propose a plan for its restoration.

Dr. Charles AnthonrProf. of Greek and Latin in Columbia College, N. Y.,—a name than which none stands higher in America for classical scholarship,—gave the following testimony, in 1843, respecting the meaning of ***baptizo,*** in a letter which has been frequently published in Baptist books on Baptism:

'There is no authority whatever for the singular remark made by the Rev. Dr. Spring relative to the force of baptizo" (viz., that in the N. T. it has no definite or distinct meaning; but "means to immerse, sprinkle, pour, and has a variety of other meanings"). "The primary meaning of the word is to dip, or immerse; and its secondary meanings, if it ever had any, all refer, in some way or other, to the same leading idea. Sprinkling, etc., are entirely out of the question."

To the same effect speaks Mr. George Wyndham,—formerly of New Orleans, one of the best scholars whom we have ever met, now, unfortunately, lost, by his residence in Europe, to America forever,—in his critical Remarks on Liddell and Scott's Greek-English Lexicon: "We are glad that Liddell and Scott have withdrawn their sanction from an interpretation wholly unwarranted. ***Bapto*** and ***baptizo*** never meant but ***to dip, to immerse, to steep.***"

Our friend and former instructor, Dr. Anthon, informed us, in the summer of 1853, that he had received numerous letters, soliciting him to withdraw the admissions made in the letter above quoted. He was told that it was doing harm to the Pædo-baptist cause, and aiding the Baptist. The Doctor, however. though himself an Episcopalian, could not renounce an opinion so manifestly correct; and very justly considered his well-earned reputation as a scholar too valuable to be sacrificed for the accomplishment of party purposes. The learned Professor has not yet withdrawn his admissions, and never will. Respecting the meaning of ***baptizo,*** he could doubtless say, with the distinguished Prof. Porson, "the Baptists have the advantage of us!"

Liddell and Scott, two eminent Pædo-baptist scholars of England, who, in the first edition of their Greek-English Lexicon, gave,—on the authority of Passow, whose Greek-German Lexicon is the basis of theirs,—***"to pour upon"*** as one of the meanings of ***"baptizo"***, have, in the second edition, withdrawn their authority for that signification; and define the word, when used literally, by ***to dip repeatedly, to sink*** (of ships), ***to bathe*** (passive), ***to baptize*** (N. T.). The significations which they now give, are substantially such as are assigned the word by Baptist scholars.

Prof. ***H. Drisler,*** of Columbia College, N. Y., who, in his first American edition of Liddell and Scott, followed their first edition, has altered the plates of his Lexicon so as to make the article on ***baptizo*** correspond to that of the second English edition. Prof. D. approves the alterations made by the English editors, and copies their article, as altered, without change, into his American edition of the Lexicon. It will so appear in all future issues of the American work,—thanks to the fairness and candor of Prof. Drisler. He, in common with other pædo-baptist critical scholars, believes that ***baptizo*** points to a "total immersion."

The authorities which follow are German.?The late Dr. Neander, of Berlin, whose fame is world-wide, from his admirable Church History, and from other valuable historico-theological writings, testifies thus in a letter to Rev. W. Judd:

'As to your question on the original rite of baptism, there can be no doubt whatever that in the primitive times it was performed by immersion, to signify a complete immersion into the new principle of the divine life which was to be imparted by the Messiah" (Judd's reply to Stuart, p. 194). To the same effect he speaks in his Church History (Rose's Translation, p. 197): "Baptism was originally administered by immersion, and many of the comparisons of St. Paul allude to this form of its administration; the immersion is a symbol of death, of being buried with Christ; the coming forth from the water is a symbol of a resurrection with Christ; and both taken together represent the second birth, the death of the old man, and a resurrection to a new life."

The Rev. Dr. Tholuck, of Halle, a staunch Lutheran, and one of the leading scholars of Germany, gives in his testimony, in these words, in his Commentary on the Romans (Eng. Trans., p. 178):

'For the explanation of this figurative description (Rom. 6: 4) of the baptismal rite, it is necessary to call attention to the well known circumstance, that, in the early days of the Church, persons, when baptized, were first plunged below, and then raised above, the water; to which practise, according to the direction of the apostle, the early Christians gave a symbolic import."

The late Dr. Olshausen, a pious, learned, and evangelical critic and theologian, speaks thus in his excellent N. T. Commentary (vol. 1, p. 158, of the German):

"It is in the highest degree probable that John's baptism resembled the Christian, not only in the fact that the baptizer performed immersion upon the one to be baptized, in which baptism differs specifically from all other lustrations, but further in the fact that, as has been remarked above, a formula was recited by the candidate."

Dr. G. C. Knapp,—whose lectures on Christian Theology, translated by Rev.

Leonard Woods, jr., have had a wide circulation in America,—makes the following admissions in favor of the Baptists (Eng. Trans., p. 486):

"Immersion is peculiarly agreeable to the institution of Christ, and the practise of the apostolic Church, and so even John baptized, and immersion remained common for a long time after; except that, in the third century, or perhaps earlier, baptism of the sick (*baptisma clinicorum*) was performed by sprinkling or affusion . . . . . By degrees, this mode of baptism became more customary, probably because it was found more convenient; especially was this the case after the seventh century, and in the Western Church, but it did not become universal until the commencement of the 14th century."

To the same effect as Dr. Knapp, speak Drs. Storr and Flatt in their Bib. Theology,—men of eminence and distinguished scholarship (bk. 4, sect. 109, ill. 4, Eng, Translation):

"The primitive mode was probably by immersion.—The disciples of our Lord could understand his commands in no other manner, than as enjoining immersion; for the baptism of John to which Jesus himself submitted, and also the earlier baptism (John 4: 1) of the disciples of Jesus, were performed by dipping the subject into cold water; as is evident from the following passages. . . . And that they actually did understand it so, is proved, partly by those passages of the New Testament which evidently allude to immersion. . . . . And partly' from the fact, that immersion was so customary in the ancient Church, that, even in the 3d century, the baptism of the sick, who were merely sprinkled with water, was entirely neglected by some, and by others was thought inferior to the baptism of those who were in health, and who received baptism, not merely by aspersion, but who actually bathed themselves in water."

Dr. K. R. Hagenbach, Prof. in Basel (Basle), has lately given the following testimony, in his "Christian Church of the First Three Centuries". It occurs in the 19th chapter, (p. 324):

"That Baptism, in the beginning, was administered in the open air, in rivers or pools, and that by immersion, is known from the narrative of the New Testament. In later times there were prepared great baptismal fonts or chapels (baptisteries). Since the person to be baptized descended several steps into the reservoir of water, and then the whole body was immersed under the water, the image of the 'burial in the death of Christ', and of 'resurrection from the grave', was impressed with power upon the soul; which, in the later practice of sprinkling, was altogether too much obscured. Sprinkling was in early times administered only to the sick, who were baptized on their dying beds, and who could not, from the circumstances of the case, be immersed."

Dr. K. R, Matthies, in his prize essay, entitled "Baptismatis Expositio" (which is a "Biblical, Historical, and Dogmatical Exposition of Baptism"), gives the following testimony, on page 116 of that able Treatise:

"Paul, as we have seen" [when speaking of Rom. 6: 3, etc.], "has in mind only the rite of immerging and submerging; and, in like manner, in the Apostolic Church, in order that communion with the death of Christ might be signified, the whole body of the person to be baptized was immersed in the water or river; and then, in order that an association with the resurrection of Christ might be indicated, the body again emerged, or was drawn forth from the water. Lamented, indeed, is it to be, that this rite, has been changed; since it places before the eyes, most fitly, the symbolical signification of baptism."

Other German authors might he cited, who speak to the same purport. We can only quote in addition, from the following:

G. W. C. Starke says, on Rom. 6: 4, in his edition of the Bible: "The apostle refers to the custom of the time,—the candidate was wholly immersed in the water, and, after he lay a short time under, was raised again. Baptism, then, is not only a striking representation of the death, but of the burial, of Christ; that, as the Lord by his burial removed the curse which lay upon him, so we become partakers of this burial, if we be plunged beneath the water as in a grave, and are covered by it."

Bretschneider, the most critical of all the N. T. lexicographers, says, in his "Theology": "An entire immersion belongs to the nature of baptism. . . . . This is the meaning of the word. . . . . In the words *baptizo* and *baptisma,* is contained the idea of a complete immersion under water; at least, so is *baptisma* in the New Testament" (vol. 2, pp. 673, 681).? *Schleusner,* —who says, that "those who were to be baptized were anciently immersed",—and *Wahl,* two other German N. T. lexicographers, limit baptism as a sacred ordinance to immersion.

Prof. Lange, in his book on Infant Baptism, says (p. 81): "Baptism in the apostolic age was a proper baptism,—the immersion of the body in water."—"Baptism consists in the immersion of the whole body in water" (***Scholz,*** on Matt. 3: 6).—"In sprinkling, the symbolical meaning of the ordinance is wholly lost" (***Rheinhard,*** Ethics, vol. 5, p. 79).—"The word ***baptize*** signifies, in Greek, sometimes to ***immerse,*** sometimes ***to sub merge"*** (***Paulus,*** N. T. Comment., vol. 1, p. 278).—"That baptism was performed, not by ***sprinkling,*** but by ***immersion,*** is evident, not only from the nature of the word, but from Rom. 6: 4" (***Fritsche,*** Comment, on Matt, 3: 6).—"The word 'baptism', according to etymology and usage, signifies to ***immerse,*** ***submerge,*** etc.; and the choice of the expression betrays an age in which the later custom of sprinkling had not been introduced" (***Augusti,*** Archæology, vol. 5, p. 5).—"Immersion in water was general until the thirteenth century; among the Latins, it was then displaced by sprinkling, but retained by the Greeks." (Von Cölln, Hist, of Doctrines, vol. 2, p. 303).—"For the sake of the sick, the rite of sprinkling was introduced" (***Gieseler,*** Ch. History, vol. 2, p. 274).—"Baptism was originally performed by immersion" (***Guericke,*** Ch. History, vol. 1, p. 116).—"John baptized at Ænon, near to Salim, because there was much water there,—enough to perform immersion" (***Dr. J. F. Von Meyer,*** on Jno. 3: 23).—"In regard to the mode (of baptism), there can he no doubt that it was not by sprinkling, but by immersion" (***Starck,*** Hist, of Baptism, p. 8).—"According to apostolic instruction and example, baptism was performed by immersing the whole man" (***Hahn,*** Theology, p. 556).—"In the apostolic age, baptism was by immersion, as its symbolical explanation shows" (***Dr. G. B. Winer,*** MSS. Lect. on Christ. Antiquities).—"Affusion was at first applied only to the sick, but was gradually introduced for others after the seventh century, and in the thirteenth became the prevailing practice in the West. But the Eastern Church has retained immersion alone as valid" (***Winer,*** MSS. Lect. on Archæology).—"In this (the first) century, baptism was administered in convenient places, without the public assemblies; and by immersing the candidate wholly in water" (***Mosheim,*** Ch. History, Am. Transl. p. 87).—Speaking of the second century, the same Author says (p. 137): "The candidates for it (baptism) were immersed wholly in water, with invocation of the sacred Trinity."

These citations are sufficient. Admissions of this kind from the best biblical critics and scholars of modern days, fortify impregnably the Baptist position. The original Greek of the New Testament teaches us that Baptism, in early times, was

Immersion. The voice of ecclesiastical history declares the same. Every version of the Scriptures, modern and ancient, in which *baptizo* and *baptisma* are translated (the Slavonic excepted, which renders *baptizo* by *krestit, to cross*), bears, up to 1820, the same positive and incontrovertible testimony. Further proof is surely unnecessary.

§2. PÆDO-BAPTIST ADMISSIONS AGAINST INFANT BAPTISM.

Shifting of the Ground of Defense of pædo-baptism—Appeal to Tradition, or to Church Authority—Bishop Taylor and the Philosopher Leibnitz give up the Argument from the Bible—The Argument from Tradition and Church Authority proved Untenable from History—Time of the Prevalence of Infant Baptism—Concessions of the North British Review, and of Dr. Bunsen—Rev. Dr. Hodge on Baptist Ground: also Rev. Drs. Stuart and Woods—Testimony of S. T. Coleridge—Admissions of German Critics and Theologians: Olshausen, Neander, Jacobi, Meyer, De Wette, and Rückert—Further Concessions: from Hagenbach, Hahn, Lange, Sehleiermacher, Von Cölin, Engelhardt, Neudecker, Münscher, Knapp, Rössler, Starck, Couard, Höfling, Winer, Rheinwald, Lindner, Dressier, Kaiser, and Baumgarten-Crusius—Testimony Conclusive—Days of Infant Baptism Numbered.

Numerous Pædo-baptist scholars have given up the direct apostolicity of Infant Baptism. In Germany, they have long done this; and, of late, the same surrender is beginning to be made in Great Britain and America. It has been found impossible to uphold the rite on the ground of its being practised in the times of the Apostles. Its advocates, therefore,—at least, the scholars among them,—are shifting the ground of their defense; but, in so doing, they yield the Protestant maxim, "the Bible, the whole Bible, and nothing but the Bible". The consequence, among "Bible Christians", may easily be predicted. Infant Baptism will gradually decrease; and it will, at last, be wholly discontinued.

Infant Baptism, it is now admitted by the most learned pædo-baptist theologians, can be defended only on the supposition of Apostolic tradition, or on that of Church authority. Having yielded the argument from the Bible, these two are the only grounds which they can plead. The eloquent Jeremy Taylor (†1667) long ago surrendered, in his "Defence of Episcopacy", the argument as drawn from the Scriptures; and based the practice, but erroneously, as we have seen, on Apostolic tradition, "The Church", he says, "has founded this rite upon the tradition of the Apostles; and wise men do easily observe that the Anabaptist can, by the same probability of Scripture, enforce a necessity of communicating infants (administering the Lord's Supper to them) upon us, as we do of baptizing infants upon them, if we speak of immediate divine institution, or of practice apostolical recorded in Scripture; and, therefore, a great master of Geneva (Calvin), in a book he writ against the Anabaptists, was forced to fly to apostolical traditive ordination."

The celebrated philosopher Leibnitz (†1716),—who "had in his life the singular felicity of being esteemed the greatest and most learned man in Europe", and who, it is added, "did not belie the public opinion",—upholds pædo-baptism in his System of Theology on the ground of Church authority. "It must be confessed," he says, "that without the authority of the Church, the baptism of children could not be adequately defended. For there is no example in its favor in the Sacred Scriptures; which appear, besides water, to demand faith also. To attribute faith, however, as some do (Luther and others), to those who cannot yet use their reason, is far too arbitrary and delusive, and quite destitute of probability. . . . . Hence, it appears to me, that *those who reject Church authority, cannot sustain the attacks of the Anabaptists."* —Never was reasoning more logical and conclusive. To make his testimony complete in favor of the Baptists, Leibnitz needed only to say, as did the English Newton, "The Baptists are the only denomination of Christians who have not symbolized with the Church of Rome."

Neither the argument from Apostolic tradition, however, nor that from Church authority, can prove the existence of Infant Baptism in the early Church; for, as has been proved, in another part of this volume, that rite was unknown in the Church until the time of Cyprian. It was not generally practiced, however, till long after his day. Even at the time of the General Council in Nice (325 A. D.), Baptist usage still prevailed; as we learn from the testimony of the historian Eusebius. That eloquent author prepared a document that met the approval of the 318 bishops assembled in the Nicene Council; according to which "instruction in the principles of Christianity in all cases preceded baptism." It reads as follows: "The exposition of our faith, as we have received it from the bishops, who were our predecessors, *both when we were first instructed in the rudiments of the faith, and when afterwards baptized into it;* as we have learned from the Holy Scriptures, and both believed and taught, not only when we sustained the office of presbyter, but since we came to the episcopal station, so do we still believe, and produce this as the account of our faith: We believe in one God," etc.

More than two centuries elapsed from the time of Cyprian, before Pædo-baptism became at all general among Christians. Up to this day, and long, after, the professed Church of Christ was, as regards the baptizing of infants, substantially Baptist. The influence of Chrysostom in the East, and of Augustine in the West, rapidly extended the erroneous and unscriptural practice. In the West, the Council of Carthage (414 A. D.) which Augustine presided, anathematized all who denied "that little children by baptism are freed from perdition and eternally saved". One hundred years later, in the beginning of the sixth century, the Emperor Justinian ordered, in the East, new-born infants to be baptized, under a penalty for neglect; "a law which", as Bunsen sadly yet truthfully remarks, "still passes for a Christian principle in the code of many a Christian state." So supported and protected, Pædo-baptism, incorrect though it is in theory and injurious in practice, acquired a foot-hold both in the East and in the West, from which neither the primitive usage up-held and kept alive from an early day, by not a few of the so-called "heretical sect", nor the earnest protests and expostulations of Baptists in modern times, have yet been able to dislodge it: but the dawn of a brighter day is lighting up the heavens, and the beginning of a new Reformation, more thoroughly evangelical than that of Luther, has burst upon the world.

The subjoined admissions of modern Pædo-baptists, coming, as they do, from the best scholarship of the age, are invaluable to Baptists. They show that the progress of Baptist principles is certain; and that they must prevail, in God's own time, throughout the whole of Christendom. Let Baptists, then, maintain, in all kindness, the baptismal discussion; and, "speaking the truth in love . . . . contend earnestly for the faith once (for all) delivered to the Saints".

In a late Article'-.("Scriptural Revision of the Litany") in the North British Review,—the organ of Presbyterianism in Scotland,—written, it is thought, by Rev. Dr. Hanna, Dr. Chalmers' son-in-law, the whole question of Infant Baptism is virtually surrendered:

"Scripture knows nothing of the baptism of infants. ***There is absolutely not a single trace of it to be found in the New Testament.*** There are passages that may be reconciled with it, if the practice can only be proved to have existed; but there is not one word which asserts its existence. . . . . . ***History confirms the inference drawn from the sacred volume.*** Infant baptism cannot be clearly traced higher than the middle of the second century; and even then it was not universal. Some, indeed, have argued that in the silence of Scripture, it is fair to presume that a custom whose existence is seen in the second century must have descended from the Apostles; ***but the presumption is wholly the other way.*** (***Aug.*** 1852.)

In another number of the same able Review (No. 37), the following Note is found: "The correctness of the picture of ancient baptism, given by Dr. Bunsen in the third volume of the present work, ["Hippolytus"] (which is indeed with more careful minuteness, just that given by Neander) ***will not, we apprehend, be disputed by any man who is content to accept the mere facts of the case.*** That the ***recognized*** baptism of the ancient Church was that of ***adults,*** of those whom the Church only received into her fold after a long course of systematic catechetical instruction, can not indeed admit of any doubt."

The testimony of Hippolytus, and of Chevalier Bunsen in his work on that Father, has been, in part, already adduced. The conclusions which Dr. Bunsen draws, admitted by Rev. Dr. Kitto and, other English biblical critics. Only one more extract from his work on "Hippolytus and his Age" will be cited here; though we should like to quote more copiously from a Pædo-baptist writer who is frank enough to say, that the Baptists "are the only evangelical community making rapid progress; and that they will always progress wherever religious life is powerfully developing itself":

"The Church ***adhered rigidly*** to the principle, as constituting the true purport of the baptism ordained by Christ,—that no one can be a member of the communion of saints, but by his own solemn vow made in the presence of the Church. It was with this understanding that the candidate for baptism was immersed in water, and admitted as a brother, upon his confession of the Father, the Son, and the Holy Ghost" (vol. 3, p. 179).

The Rev. Dr. Hodge, Professor in Princeton Theological Seminary, who is one of the firmest upholders and defenders of Presbyterianism (O. S.) in America, takes Baptist ground, in the Princeton Review (Oct. '52), respecting the Abrahamic Covenant and the relation of the Church to the world. His arguments,—which he brings to bear against Episcopalianism,—may be turned with deadly effect against Infant Baptism, on whatever ground, and by whomsoever advocated. Such admissions as the subjoined, are fatal to Pædo-baptism in any sense:

"*When Christ came, the commonwealth was abolished, and there was nothing put in its place.* The Church remained. There was no external covenant, nor promises of external blessings, on condition of external rites and subjection. There was a spiritual society, with spiritual promises, *on the condition of faith in Christ, In no part of the New Testament, is any other condition of membership in the Church prescribed than that contained in the answer of Philip to the eunuch who desired baptism:* 'If thou believest with all thy heart, thou mayest. And he answered and said, I believe that Jesus Christ is the Son of God.' The Church, therefore, is, in its essential nature, *a company of believers;* and not an external society, requiring merely external profession as the condition of membership."

Prof. *Moses Stuart,* of Andover, yields, as does Dr. Hodge, the argument from circumcision, when he says (Old Testament, Ch. 22): "How unwary, too, are many excellent men, in contending for infant baptism on the ground of the Jewish analogy of circumcision! . . . . Numberless difficulties present themselves in our way, as soon as we begin to argue in such a manner as this." The same distinguished Professor candidly admits that, as to infant baptism, he can not "find commands, or plain and certain examples, in the New Testament relative to it". And Rev. *Dr. Woods,* also, an eminent writer on the Pædo-baptist side, says distinctly, "We have no express precept or example for infant baptism in all our holy Writings."

The late S. T. Coleridge, an admirable scholar, and one of the deepest thinkers that England has ever produced, exposes the fallacy of the argument for Pædo-baptism, as drawn from the N. T. mention of the baptism of households:

"Had baptism of infants at that early period of the Gospel been a known practice, or had this been previously demonstrated, then, indeed, the argument that in all probability there was one or more infants or young children in so large a family, would be no otherwise objectionable than as being superfluous, and a sort of anti-climax in logic. But if the words are cited as *the* proof, it would be a clear *petitio principii,* though there had been nothing else against it. . . . Equally vain is the pretended analogy from circumcision, which was no sacrament at all, but the means and mark of national distinction. . . . . (Historically considered) there exists no sufficient positive evidence that the baptism of infants was instituted by the Apostles in the practice of the Apostolic Age" (Works, Am. edit. vol. 1, p. 335–337)[19].

The most distinguished theologians and critics yield, without hesitation, the apostolicity, though they approve and defend the practice, of Infant Baptism. Indeed, it would be difficult to mention any late acknowledged German authority, who does not at once concede this point to the Baptists.

Olshausen makes the following admissions in his N. T. Commentary. On Matt. 19: 14, speaking of the children brought to Christ, he says: "Of the reference to infant baptism which is often sought for in this narrative, there is evidently no trace. The Saviour represents the children to the Apostles as the symbol of the spiritual second birth and the childlike disposition bestowed in it. On the part of the parents who brought the children, there was clearly nothing expected for them, but a spiritual blessing (by which baptism is by no means to be supposed), and this the little ones obtained by the laying on of Christ's hands, which, in connection with the prayer by which it was accompanied, could not have been devoid of a beneficial spiritual influence."—On 1 Cor. 7: 14, he remarks briefly and pointedly: "It is, moreover, clear that Paul would not have chosen this argument, had infant baptism been practised at the time."—Respecting the baptism of Lydia and her household, he says, on Acts 16: 14, 15: "Baptism ensued in this case, without doubt, only upon the profession of faith in Jesus as the Messiah. On this very account it is in the highest degree improbable that by 'her house' is to be understood children under age. Relatives, servants, grown-up children, were baptized with her, because they had been convinced by the youthful power of her new life of faith. We can not, in truth, find any where, a reliable proof-text in favor of infant baptism in apostolic times; and its necessity is not deducible from the design of baptism."

Neander admits, in several of his writings, that infant baptism can not be proved to have existed in the age of the Apostles. We need quote but sparingly: "As

---

19 The baptism of households,—entire families,—upon repentance and faith, is not uncommon in our day. Before the Karen Baptist mission was as old as the Apostolic mission, at the time Lydia was baptized, there belonged to it *eight* baptized families. At present, it is said, there are more than *thirty* such. Numerous baptized believing families are found in America.

faith and baptism are constantly so closely connected together in the New Testament, an opinion was likely to arise, that where there could be no faith there could also be no baptism. It is certain that Christ did not ordain infant baptism. . . . . We cannot prove that the apostles ordained infant baptism; from those places where the baptism of a whole family is mentioned, as in Acts 16: 33, 1 Cor. 1: 16, we can draw no such conclusion, because the inquiry is still to be made, whether there were any children in these families of such an age, that they were not capable of any intelligent conception of Christianity; for this is the only point on which the case turns." (Ch. History Rose's Trans., p. 198).—In his "Planting and Training," (Ryland's Trans., p. 101), Neander writes as follows: "Since baptism marked the entrance into communion with Christ, it resulted, from *the nature* of the rite, that a *confession of faith* in Jesus, as the Redeemer, would be made by the person to be baptized; and in the latter part of the *apostolic* age, we may find indications of the existence of such a practise. As baptism was closely united with a *conscious* entrance on Christian communion, *faith and baptism were always connected,* and thus it is in the highest degree probable that baptism was performed only in the instances when *both could meet* together, and that the practise of *infant baptism was unknown* at this period" (the apostolic age).

Prof. *J. L. Jacobi,* of Berlin, who is himself writing a Church History, agrees with his friend Neander, in his Article on "Baptism", published in Dr. Kitto's Bib. Cyclopædia: "Infant baptism was established neither by Christ, nor the Apostles. In all places where we find the necessity of baptism notified, either in a dogmatic or historical point of view, it is evident it was only meant for those who were capable of comprehending the word preached, and of being converted to Christ by an act of their own will. A pretty sure testimony of its non-existence in the apostolic age may be inferred from 1 Cor. 7: 14, since Paul would certainly have referred to the baptism of children for their holiness. . . . . In support of the contrary opinion, the advocates in former ages (now hardly any) used to appeal to Matt. 19: 14; but their strongest argument in its favor is the regulation of baptizing all the members of a house and family (1 Cor. 16: 15; Acts 16: 33; 18: 8). In none of these instances has it been proved that there were little children among them; but, even if there were, there was no necessity for excluding them from baptism in plain words, since such exclusion was understood as a matter of course."

Dr. *H. A. W. Meyer*, whose Commentary on the New Testament is a very scholarly performance,—in some respects the best ever published,—speaks thus on Acts 16: 15: "Appeal is made to this passage to 18: 8, and 1 Cor. 1: 16, in order to prove the custom of infant baptism in the Apostolic age, or, at least, to show its probability; but without reason. For that the baptism of children was not in use at that time appears evident from 1 Cor. 7: 14; where Paul could not have written, 'Else were your children unclean, but now they are holy,' if the children had been ecclesiastically holy by virtue of their baptism."

The late Dr. *W. M. L. De Wette*—whose N. T. Commentary is a monument of learning and research,—remarks as follows on Acts 16: 15; "This passage as well as verse 33, 18: 8, 1 Cor. 1: 16, has been adduced in proof of the apostolical authority of infant baptism; but there is no evidence here that any except adults were baptized." On 1 Cor. 7: 14, De Wette agrees with Dr. Meyer. He thinks that the text proves that the baptism of children was not known in the primitive churches. "In this passage, therefore," he says, "we have a proof that children had not begun to be baptized in the time of the Apostles." This opinion is expressed by him in an Article on Baptism, in the "Studien und Kritiken", for 1830 (p. 669).—Dr. Rückert, on 1 Cor. 7: 14, says: "It is plain that De Wette and Neander have with reason regarded the passage as proof that the baptism of children did not exist in the time of Paul."

In citing from other authorities, we must be more brief.?"Infant baptism had not come into general use prior to the time of Tertullian. . . . The passages from the Scripture which are thought to prove that infant baptism had come into use are doubtful and prove nothing" (*Hagenbach,* Hist, of Doctrines, pp. 190, 193);— "Baptism, according to its original design, can be given only to adults who are capable of true knowledge, repentance, and faith. Neither in the Scripture, nor during the first hundred and fifty years, is a sure example of infant baptism to be found; and we must concede that the numerous opposers of it, cannot be contradicted on Gospel grounds" (*Hahn,* Theology, p. 556).—"All attempts to make out infant baptism from the N. T. fail; it is totally opposed to the spirit of the Apostolic age, and to the fundamental principles of the New Testament" (*Prof. Lange,* Infant Baptism, p, 101).—"Baptism is only then complete and right, when it is performed under the same conditions, with *the same spiritual pre-requisites* and the same influences, as were found in those who were baptized in primitive times" (*Schleiermacher,* Dogmatik, vol. 2, p. 540).—"That Jesus required this [previous instruction] is shown in. Mark 16: 15, where he makes the announcing of doctrine to precede baptism. It is involved in this, that baptism can be fulfilled on those only who are capable of instruction, or only on adults; and that it was certainly not the design of Jesus to introduce infant baptism" (Von Cölln, Bib. Theology, vol. 2, p. 145).—"Infant baptism was not yet customary in the first two centuries" (***Engelhardt,*** Hist. of Doctrines, vol. 1, p. 333).—"Originally, none were baptized except adults who had received instruction in the Christian religion, and were called catechumens" (***Neudecker,*** Lexicon of Ch. Hist., Art. Baptism).—"All the earlier traces of infant baptism are very doubtful. Tertullian is the first who refers to it; and he censures it" (Münscher, Hist. of Doctrines, vol. 1, p. 469).—"There is no decisive example of this practise in the N. T. . . . . There is, therefore, no express command for infant baptism" (***Knapp,*** Theology, Eng. Transl., p. 494).

Prof. Lange, of Jena, already cited once, speaks to the point in his Hist. of Protestantism (pp. 34, 35): "Would the Protestant Church fulfil and attain to its final destiny, the baptism of new-born children must of necessity be abolished. It has sunk down to a mere formality, without any religious meaning for the child; and stands in direct contradiction to the fundamental doctrines of the Reformers on the advantage and use of the sacraments. It can not from any point of view be justified by the Holy Scriptures." One would suppose the writer to be a Baptist did he not know to the contrary. The Professor remarks, in another place, "The baptism of newborn children was altogether unknown to primitive Christianity" (p. 221).

"So far as I have hitherto perused the Fathers, no clear and certain proof has come before me adequate to establish it [i. e. infant baptism], prior to Origen; although there are a few passages which render it not without probability" (Rössler, Christ. Church in the First Three Centuries, p. 299).—"It can not be denied that no example can be cited from the books of the N. T. that the apostles and disciples of the Lord baptized children and babes" (***Starch,*** Hist, of Baptism, p. 10). To the same effect speaks ***Dr. Couard,*** in his Life of the Early Christians (Eng. Trans., p. 202); and Prof. Höfling, in his sacrament of Baptism) vol. 1, pp. 99,104).—"Originally, only adults were baptized; but, at the end of the second century, in Africa, and in the third century, generally, infant baptism was introduced; and, in the fourth century, it was theologically maintained by Augustine" (***Winer,*** MSB. Lectures). So ***Rheinwald*** speaks of the rite as not becoming "a general ecclesiastical institution till the age of Augustine".—"Christian baptism can be given only to adults, not to infants. The Holy Spirit, which is given only to believers, was a pre-requisite to baptism" (***Prof. Lindner,*** Lord's Supper, p. 123).—"In the N. T., the consecration by baptism always relates to those only whose faith was changed, and who were made acquainted with Christ, and became his disciples" (***Dressier,*** Baptism, p. 137).— "Infant baptism was not an original institution of Christianity. . . . . The first traces are in the second century" (***Kaiser,*** Bib. Theology, vol. 2, p. 178).—"Infant baptism can be supported, neither by a distinct apostolical tradition, nor apostolical practice" (***Baumgarten-Crusius,*** Hist. of Theology p. 1208).

Testimonies such as have been cited against Infant Baptism, as un-apostolic and non-primitive, can not wisely be disregarded. Some of them come from biblical scholars who have never been equalled in any age, for thorough research and extensive and sound learning; men of vast and profound erudition, whose ecclesiastical prepossessions would lead them to speak otherwise, but who, in the spirit of true scholarship, judge every question upon its intrinsic merits, draw their conclusions impartially and honestly, in accordance with the well-established canons of criticism and logic.

Before such testimony Infant Baptism can not stand. False in theory and wrong in practice, it is destined to die. Where not supported by State authority, or sustained by the belief that baptism regenerates the soul, in some magical way, and independent of the mental condition of the candidate, it is even now decreasing. It will continue to decline, for the finger of God has written upon its front, "***Mene, mene, tekel, upharsin***"

§3. PROOF OF BELIEVERS' IMMERSION FROM THE ANCIENT BAPTISTERIES AND FONTS.

First Baptisms in Rivers, Pools, and Baths—Baptisteries introduced in the Fourth Century—Description of a Baptistery—Names applied to the Building—Object of the Baptisteries—Notices of several Ancient, chiefly Italian, Baptisteries—The Baptismal Fonts—Size of the Fonts?Notices of the Fonts in the Baptisteries already mentioned—Even Infants in later times, Dipped—Notices of several

Ancient Fonts—Fonts in the English Churches—Immersion in these Fonts—The Fonts of Italy meant for Immersion—Returning to the Simplicity of the Apostolic and Primitive Church.

A strong argument in favor of the position that Believers' immersion alone was considered Baptism in the Apostolic and in the early Church, has been founded upon the size and structure of the ancient Baptisteries and Fonts. In the first centuries of Christianity, down at least until the middle of the third, baptism was performed in any convenient place,—in rivers, pools, and baths. John the Baptist, and Christ's disciples, baptized in the Jordan. Philip baptized the eunuch in a stream or pool upon the public road; and Peter, Tertullian asserts, performed the rite in the river Tiber. Clement, of Borne, says that a river, or fountain, or the sea, is, according to circumstances, a suitable place for administering the Christian ordinance. In Justin Martyr's time, the candidates were led "to some place where there was water". Tertullian declares "that it is immaterial where a person is baptized, whether in the sea, or in standing or running water, a fountain, lake, or river".

About the time of Constantine, however, in the beginning of the fourth century, chapels or halls, called *Baptisteries,* began to be built, for the administration of the ordinance. These Baptisteries were connected with the *cathedral churches,* only one of which was allowed in each episcopal diocese; from which circumstance they were sometimes called *baptismal churches* ("ecclesias baptismales"). Such "baptismal churches" were generally built near rivers, or waters, as at Milan, Naples, Ravenna, Verona, etc., in Italy.

The baptistery was a building separate from the church, but often connected with it by a covered passage-way. In shape, it was, almost always, either round or octagonal, with a cupola roof resembling the dome of a cathedral. "All the middle part of this building was," as Robinson says, "one large hall, capable of containing a great multitude of people: the sides were parted off, and divided into rooms; and, in some, rooms were added without the sides, in the fashion of cloisters."

The entire baptistery, from being used as a place for giving instruction to candidates for the Christian rite (catechumens) was often called a *photisterion,*—a place for giving light, an *illuminatory.* Sometimes it was styled a *school,* sometimes a *hall* (*aula*); names indicating a place where believers were prepared for baptism,—for here the candidates for the rite received instruction, before the reception of the ordinance, in the leading principles of the Christian religion.

These ancient baptisteries,—in which alone it is worthy of remark, baptism was, by special order, allowed to be performed as early as the time of Justinian (†565),—were evidently intended for the immersion of adults. Baptism, at this time was, in general, administered only twice a year, at Easter and at Whitsuntide, sometimes at Christmas; and on these occasions a goodly number often received the ordinance. The baptisteries needed, therefore, to be large. Joseph Bingham (†1723), a learned Episcopalian writer, has the following on this point in his "Eccles. Antiquities": "These baptisteries were anciently very capacious, because, as Dr. Cave truly observes, the stated times of baptism returning but seldom, there were usually great numbers to be baptized at the same time.—And then, *the manner of baptizing by immersion or the dipping under water made it necessary to have a large font likewise.* Whence the author of the Alexandrian Chronicle styles the baptistery whither Basilicus fled to take sanctuary, the great illuminary or school of baptism. And in Venantius Fortunatus it is called *aula baptismatis,* the large hall of baptism; which was indeed so capacious that we sometimes read of councils meeting and sitting therein, as Du Fresne shows out of the acts of the Council of Chalcedon, and Suicerus has observed the same in the acts of the Council of Carthage, which speaks of a Council at Constantinople held in the baptistery of the church" (p. 309).

The baptistery of St. Sophia, in Constantinople, erected by Constantine (†337), adorned by succeeding Emperors, and rebuilt by Justinian, was a large and splendid edifice. It was so spacious that Councils were held in it. In the centre, as in other baptisteries, was the pool for baptizing; supplied with water by pipes, and having every convenience for immersion.—The baptistery near the church of St. John of Lateran, in Rome, (built about 324 A. D.) is an octagonal building, sixty-four feet in-diameter; the roof of which is supported by "eight large polygonal pillars of porphyry".—At Ravenna, Italy, there are two baptisteries: the one built in the time of Valentinian (†375), and repaired by Neo, Archbishop of Ravenna, in 451; the other built in the reign of Theodoric (†526). The former is an octagonal building, about thirty-two feet square inside; having a dome supported by eight marble pillars, and "ornamented with mosaic work of the utmost magnificence." In the middle of the dome is a representation of the baptism of Christ in the Jordan. Jesus is pictured standing in the river, waist-deep in water.—The baptistery of Florence is still a remarkable edifice: in the year 1300, it was "a most elegant building, and highly ornamented". On its floor were several baths, where at Easter, baptism was administered by immersion.—The baptistery in Pisa is a circular building, of white marble, measuring 115 feet in diameter, and 172 feet in height. It is often called "the glory of Pisa".

The ancient Baptisteries, as has been seen, were buildings, not fonts. But they contained fonts. In the middle of each baptistery was the bath or pool, in which the Christian ordinance was administered. It was usually constructed of stone; and the descent into it was by three steps. Over the pool hovered, in the larger baptisteries, a dove of gold or silver,——a symbol of the Holy Spirit. The bath was called by the Greeks ***kolumbethra, a swimming or bathing place;*** equivalent to the Latin ***natatoria*** and ***lavacrum.*** By the Latins, it was sometimes called ***fons,*** the ***font;*** sometimes ***pisceria*** (literally, the ***fish-pond***), a name which has reference to the symbolical use of the Greek word for ***fish,*** the letters of which form the initials of the Greek expression for "Jesus Christ, Son of God, Saviour."

These and other names given to the fonts in the baptisteries, show that reservoirs of water are described; artificial basins in which immersion was performed. In subsequent ages, when infant baptism had become general, the size of the fonts was reduced; but, "in primitive times", as Charles Wheatley (†1742), the Episcopalian, correctly says, in his work on the "Book of Common Prayer", "we meet with them very large and capacious, not only that they might comport with the general customs of those times, viz., of persons being immersed or put under water, but also because the stated times of baptism returning so seldom, great numbers were usually baptized at the same time. In the middle of them was always a partition, the one part for men, the other for women; that so, by being baptized asunder, they might avoid giving offence and scandal. But immersion being now too generally discontinued, they have shrunk into little small fonts, scarce bigger than mortars, and only employed to hold less basins with water, though this last be expressly contrary to an ancient advertisement of our Church" (p. 337).

The font,—"an immense porphyry vase",—in the baptistery of the Lateran at Rome, is "somewhat over three feet" deep, and is lined and paved with marble. In the centre of this, another font, of modern origin, constructed of basalt, now stands on marble steps.—In the Valentinian baptistery in Ravenna, the font is an octagonal bath of white Grecian marble and porphyry, about nine feet square. At its farther end is a marble pulpit, overlooking the water.—The font at Pisa is octangular, with four small fonts in the angles. In its centre stands a statue of John the Baptist. "The font", remarks one who has visited it, "is quite capacious,—from three to four feet deep, and sufficiently wide to admit of the immersion of the largest persons."—The font in the baptistery in Parma, made of marble, is four feet deep, and five or six in diameter.

In the first baptisteries, both the administrator and the candidate generally went down into the bath; but, when infant baptism became common, the administrator, having no need, did not go into the water. But the candidates were still dipped. Even infants were, until a comparatively late period, immersed; and the later fonts were constructed with an eye to this fact. "All fonts", as Robinson says, "fixed and moveable, were intended for the administration of baptism by dipping." Many of these old fonts, some of which still exist, are remarkable.

In a font belonging to the church of Notre Dame, Paris, Clovis, (†511) the first Christian king of the Franks, was immersed on Christmas eve. He was baptized by being dipped three times. Audofledis, his sister, received the rite at the same time and in the same manner.—In Milan, Italy, fonts are still extant, which were, centuries since, consecrated to baptismal purposes, and are still regularly and habitually employed for immersing recipients of the baptismal ordinance. The Ambrosian ritual, which is more ancient than the Roman liturgy, positively requires "baptism by immersion".—The font in the baptistery of St. John of Lateran,—in which some think, but on insufficient grounds, that Constantine was immersed,—is still used, occasionally, on the Saturday before Easter, for baptizing converted infidels and Jews."—The oldest church in Lyons, France, is said to have "recently restored the baptistery long destroyed".

In England, the first missionaries from Rome baptized in rivers. Austin did so. Paulinus immersed in the rivers Glen and Swale. Edwin, however, the king of Northumberland, was baptized by the same Paulinus, in a font within "a wooden booth at York".

England never had baptisteries. Some of the parish churches, however, still contain the fonts which were in by-gone days, up to the time of James I., regularly used for dipping. In the old church of St. Peter, Oxford, there was, not many years since, "a very ancient baptismal font", eleven feet in circumference, and proportionally deep.—In the Bridekirk church, in Cumberland, there is a Danish font, of greenish stone. The baptism of Christ is represented on the east side. Jesus stands unclothed, "in a kind of font or vase", with John the Baptist, on his right, in the act of performing the baptismal ordinance.—The oldest English font is said to be that of St. Martin's church, Canterbury. It is shaped like a tub, is three feet high, and capacious within. It is thought by some to have been constructed by Christians in the Roman army, somewhere about 187 A. D.; and to have been the font in which Ethelbert, the Saxon king, was baptized. This is not probable, however; for Bede, the historian, tells us that Ethelbert was "washed" in the river Swale; and makes no mention of fonts at this early period.

Immersion in fonts did not fall into disuse in England until the time of the Stuarts. Edward VI. and Queen Elizabeth were both, when infants, baptized publicly, in a font, by trine immersion.

One of the old English fonts was restored to its ancient use a year or two ago, in the Bradford parish church; a young lady having been immersed, by Rev. Dr. Burnet, in "the large stone font, weighing several tons, which is usually kept under the tower".

All that we know of the ancient baptisteries and fonts goes to prove that, for many centuries, immersion alone, even among the Christians of the West, was considered baptism; and thus confirms the results which we have reached by other and more direct and convincing considerations. Pædo-baptists sometimes appeal to the size and form of the ancient baptisteries and fonts, in support of their views on baptism. It seemed well to remove this prop, also, from beneath the tottering edifice of their argumentation.

"The traveler", it has been well said by one who has seen the baptisteries of Italy, "who stands and muses beside these monuments of by-gone days, will seldom be so blinded by prejudice as to suppose that they were erected for any other purpose than the immersion of the candidates who sought admission to the church. These baptisteries bear decisive testimony to the mode of baptism which prevailed [even in the West], from the fourth to the fourteenth century. Their origin is to be traced to different eras during that period of a thousand years."

The Roman Catholic Church has corrupted the act, as well as changed the subjects, of Baptism; but, in these baptisteries,—apart from their own admissions,—she has preserved for us monuments that point back to the original ordinance, simple and unchanged, as in Apostolic times. "May they long stand", say we, in the forcible language of another; "stand, at least, till their mute testimony shall be duly regarded, and those who love not the errors of the Church of Rome, come also to be unflinching and consistent Protestants against the change which she has wrought in this ordinance of the Gospel." God speed the coming of the day in which the Church of his Son shall prosper in every land; and shine forth, pure and spotless, "as a bride adorned for her husband".

The Codes Of Hammurabi And Moses
W. W. Davies

QTY

The discovery of the Hammurabi Code is one of the greatest achievements of archaeology, and is of paramount interest, not only to the student of the Bible, but also to all those interested in ancient history...

Religion   **ISBN:** *1-59462-338-4*   **Pages:132**
MSRP $12.95

The Theory of Moral Sentiments
Adam Smith

QTY

This work from 1749. contains original theories of conscience amd moral judgment and it is the foundation for systemof morals.

Philosophy **ISBN:** *1-59462-777-0*   **Pages:536**
MSRP $19.95

Jessica's First Prayer
Hesba Stretton

QTY

In a screened and secluded corner of one of the many railway-bridges which span the streets of London there could be seen a few years ago, from five o'clock every morning until half past eight, a tidily set-out coffee-stall, consisting of a trestle and board, upon which stood two large tin cans, with a small fire of charcoal burning under each so as to keep the coffee boiling during the early hours of the morning when the work-people were thronging into the city on their way to their daily toil...

Pages:84

Childrens   **ISBN:** *1-59462-373-2*   *MSRP $9.95*

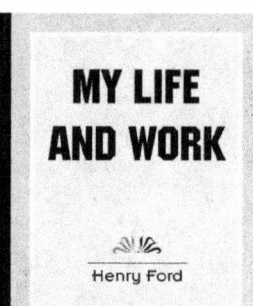

My Life and Work
Henry Ford

QTY

Henry Ford revolutionized the world with his implementation of mass production for the Model T automobile. Gain valuable business insight into his life and work with his own auto-biography... "We have only started on our development of our country we have not as yet, with all our talk of wonderful progress, done more than scratch the surface. The progress has been wonderful enough but..."

Pages:300

Biographies/   **ISBN:** *1-59462-198-5*   *MSRP $21.95*

www.bookjungle.com *email: sales@bookjungle.com fax: 630-214-0564 mail: Book Jungle PO Box 2226 Champaign, IL 61825*

The Art of Cross-Examination
Francis Wellman

QTY

I presume it is the experience of every author, after his first book is published upon an important subject, to be almost overwhelmed with a wealth of ideas and illustrations which could readily have been included in his book, and which to his own mind, at least, seem to make a second edition inevitable. Such certainly was the case with me; and when the first edition had reached its sixth impression in five months, I rejoiced to learn that it seemed to my publishers that the book had met with a sufficiently favorable reception to justify a second and considerably enlarged edition. ..

Pages:412

Reference   **ISBN: *1-59462-647-2***   *MSRP $19.95*

On the Duty of Civil Disobedience
Henry David Thoreau

QTY

Thoreau wrote his famous essay, On the Duty of Civil Disobedience, as a protest against an unjust but popular war and the immoral but popular institution of slave-owning. He did more than write—he declined to pay his taxes, and was hauled off to gaol in consequence. Who can say how much this refusal of his hastened the end of the war and of slavery ?

Law   **ISBN: *1-59462-747-9***   **Pages:48**

MSRP $7.45

Dream Psychology Psychoanalysis for Beginners
Sigmund Freud

QTY

Sigmund Freud, born Sigismund Schlomo Freud (May 6, 1856 - September 23, 1939), was a Jewish-Austrian neurologist and psychiatrist who co-founded the psychoanalytic school of psychology. Freud is best known for his theories of the unconscious mind, especially involving the mechanism of repression; his redefinition of sexual desire as mobile and directed towards a wide variety of objects; and his therapeutic techniques, especially his understanding of transference in the therapeutic relationship and the presumed value of dreams as sources of insight into unconscious desires.

Pages:196

Psychology   **ISBN: *1-59462-905-6***   *MSRP $15.45*

The Miracle of Right Thought
Orison Swett Marden

QTY

Believe with all of your heart that you will do what you were made to do. When the mind has once formed the habit of holding cheerful, happy, prosperous pictures, it will not be easy to form the opposite habit. It does not matter how improbable or how far away this realization may see, or how dark the prospects may be, if we visualize them as best we can, as vividly as possible, hold tenaciously to them and vigorously struggle to attain them, they will gradually become actualized, realized in the life. But a desire, a longing without endeavor, a yearning abandoned or held indifferently will vanish without realization.

Pages:360

Self Help   **ISBN: *1-59462-644-8***   *MSRP $25.45*

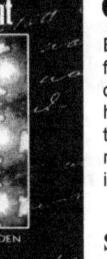

QTY

☐ **The Rosicrucian Cosmo-Conception Mystic Christianity** *by Max Heindel*   ISBN: *1-59462-188-8* **$38.95**
The Rosicrucian Cosmo-conception is not dogmatic, neither does it appeal to any other authority than the reason of the student. It is not controversial, but is: sent forth in the, hope that it may help to clear...   New Age/Religion Pages 646

☐ **Abandonment To Divine Providence** *by Jean-Pierre de Caussade*   ISBN: *1-59462-228-0* **$25.95**
"The Rev. Jean Pierre de Caussade was one of the most remarkable spiritual writers of the Society of Jesus in France in the 18th Century. His death took place at Toulouse in 1751. His works have gone through many editions and have been republished...   Inspirational/Religion Pages 400

☐ **Mental Chemistry** *by Charles Haanel*   ISBN: *1-59462-192-6* **$23.95**
Mental Chemistry allows the change of material conditions by combining and appropriately utilizing the power of the mind. Much like applied chemistry creates something new and unique out of careful combinations of chemicals the mastery of mental chemistry...   New Age Pages 354

☐ **The Letters of Robert Browning and Elizabeth Barret Barrett 1845-1846 vol II**   ISBN: *1-59462-193-4* **$35.95**
by Robert Browning and Elizabeth Barrett   Biographies Pages 596

☐ **Gleanings In Genesis (volume I)** *by Arthur W. Pink*   ISBN: *1-59462-130-6* **$27.45**
Appropriately has Genesis been termed "the seed plot of the Bible" for in it we have, in germ form, almost all of the great doctrines which are afterwards fully developed in the books of Scripture which follow...   Religion/Inspirational Pages 420

☐ **The Master Key** *by L. W. de Laurence*   ISBN: *1-59462-001-6* **$30.95**
In no branch of human knowledge has there been a more lively increase of the spirit of research during the past few years than in the study of Psychology, Concentration and Mental Discipline. The requests for authentic lessons in Thought Control, Mental Discipline and...   New Age/Business Pages 422

☐ **The Lesser Key Of Solomon Goetia** *by L. W. de Laurence*   ISBN: *1-59462-092-X* **$9.95**
This translation of the first book of the "Lernegton" which is now for the first time made accessible to students of Talismanic Magic was done, after careful collation and edition, from numerous Ancient Manuscripts in Hebrew, Latin, and French...   New Age/Occult Pages 92

☐ **Rubaiyat Of Omar Khayyam** *by Edward Fitzgerald*   ISBN:*1-59462-332-5* **$13.95**
Edward Fitzgerald, whom the world has already learned, in spite of his own efforts to remain within the shadow of anonymity, to look upon as one of the rarest poets of the century, was born at Bredfield, in Suffolk, on the 31st of March, 1809. He was the third son of John Purcell...   Music Pages 172

☐ **Ancient Law** *by Henry Maine*   ISBN: *1-59462-128-4* **$29.95**
The chief object of the following pages is to indicate some of the earliest ideas of mankind, as they are reflected in Ancient Law, and to point out the relation of those ideas to modern thought.   Religion/History Pages 452

☐ **Far-Away Stories** *by William J. Locke*   ISBN: *1-59462-129-2* **$19.45**
"Good wine needs no bush, but a collection of mixed vintages does. And this book is just such a collection. Some of the stories I do not want to remain buried for ever in the museum files of dead magazine-numbers an author's not unpardonable vanity..."   Fiction Pages 272

☐ **Life of David Crockett** *by David Crockett*   ISBN: *1-59462-250-7* **$27.45**
"Colonel David Crockett was one of the most remarkable men of the times in which he lived. Born in humble life, but gifted with a strong will, an indomitable courage, and unremitting perseverance...   Biographies/New Age Pages 424

☐ **Lip-Reading** *by Edward Nitchie*   ISBN: *1-59462-206-X* **$25.95**
Edward B. Nitchie, founder of the New York School for the Hard of Hearing, now the Nitchie School of Lip-Reading, Inc, wrote "LIP-READING Principles and Practice". The development and perfecting of this meritorious work on lip-reading was an undertaking...   How-to Pages 400

☐ **A Handbook of Suggestive Therapeutics, Applied Hypnotism, Psychic Science**   ISBN: *1-59462-214-0* **$24.95**
by Henry Munro   Health/New Age/Health/Self-help Pages 376

☐ **A Doll's House: and Two Other Plays** *by Henrik Ibsen*   ISBN: *1-59462-112-8* **$19.95**
Henrik Ibsen created this classic when in revolutionary 1848 Rome. Introducing some striking concepts in playwriting for the realist genre, this play has been studied the world over.   Fiction/Classics/Plays 308

☐ **The Light of Asia** *by sir Edwin Arnold*   ISBN: *1-59462-204-3* **$13.95**
In this poetic masterpiece, Edwin Arnold describes the life and teachings of Buddha. The man who was to become known as Buddha to the world was born as Prince Gautama of India but he rejected the worldly riches and abandoned the reigns of power when...   Religion/History/Biographies Pages 170

☐ **The Complete Works of Guy de Maupassant** *by Guy de Maupassant*   ISBN: *1-59462-157-8* **$16.95**
"For days and days, nights and nights, I had dreamed of that first kiss which was to consecrate our engagement, and I knew not on what spot I should put my lips..."   Fiction/Classics Pages 240

☐ **The Art of Cross-Examination** *by Francis L. Wellman*   ISBN: *1-59462-309-0* **$26.95**
Written by a renowned trial lawyer, Wellman imparts his experience and uses case studies to explain how to use psychology to extract desired information through questioning.   How-to/Science/Reference Pages 408

☐ **Answered or Unanswered?** *by Louisa Vaughan*   ISBN: *1-59462-248-5* **$10.95**
Miracles of Faith in China   Religion Pages 112

☐ **The Edinburgh Lectures on Mental Science (1909)** *by Thomas*   ISBN: *1-59462-008-3* **$11.95**
This book contains the substance of a course of lectures recently given by the writer in the Queen Street Hall, Edinburgh. Its purpose is to indicate the Natural Principles governing the relation between Mental Action and Material Conditions...   New Age/Psychology Pages 148

☐ **Ayesha** *by H. Rider Haggard*   ISBN: *1-59462-301-5* **$24.95**
Verily and indeed it is the unexpected that happens! Probably if there was one person upon the earth from whom the Editor of this, and of a certain previous history, did not expect to hear again...   Classics Pages 380

☐ **Ayala's Angel** *by Anthony Trollope*   ISBN: *1-59462-352-X* **$29.95**
The two girls were both pretty, but Lucy who was twenty-one who supposed to be simple and comparatively unattractive, whereas Ayala was credited, as her Bombwhat romantic name show, with poetic charm and a taste for romance. Ayala when her father died was nineteen...   Fiction Pages 484

☐ **The American Commonwealth** *by James Bryce*   ISBN: *1-59462-286-8* **$34.45**
An interpretation of American democratic political theory. It examines political mechanics and society from the perspective of Scotsman James Bryce   Politics Pages 572

☐ **Stories of the Pilgrims** *by Margaret P. Pumphrey*   ISBN: *1-59462-116-0* **$17.95**
This book explores pilgrims religious oppression in England as well as their escape to Holland and eventual crossing to America on the Mayflower, and their early days in New England...   History Pages 268

QTY

The Fasting Cure *by Sinclair Upton*　　　　　ISBN: *1-59462-222-1*　**$13.95**
In the Cosmopolitan Magazine for May, 1910, and in the Contemporary Review (London) for April, 1910, I published an article dealing with my experiences in fasting. I have written a great many magazine articles, but never one which attracted so much attention... New Age/Self Help/Health Pages 164

Hebrew Astrology *by Sepharial*　　　　　ISBN: *1-59462-308-2*　**$13.45**
In these days of advanced thinking it is a matter of common observation that we have left many of the old landmarks behind and that we are now pressing forward to greater heights and to a wider horizon than that which represented the mind-content of our progenitors... Astrology Pages 144

Thought Vibration or The Law of Attraction in the Thought World　　ISBN: *1-59462-127-6*　**$12.95**

by William Walker Atkinson　　　　　　　　　Psychology/Religion Pages 144

Optimism *by Helen Keller*　　　　　ISBN: *1-59462-108-X*　**$15.95**
Helen Keller was blind, deaf, and mute since 19 months old, yet famously learned how to overcome these handicaps, communicate with the world, and spread her lectures promoting optimism. An inspiring read for everyone... Biographies/Inspirational Pages 84

Sara Crewe *by Frances Burnett*　　　　　ISBN: *1-59462-360-0*　**$9.45**
In the first place, Miss Minchin lived in London. Her home was a large, dull, tall one, in a large, dull square, where all the houses were alike, and all the sparrows were alike, and where all the door-knockers made the same heavy sound... Childrens/Classic Pages 88

The Autobiography of Benjamin Franklin *by Benjamin Franklin*　　ISBN: *1-59462-135-7*　**$24.95**
The Autobiography of Benjamin Franklin has probably been more extensively read than any other American historical work, and no other book of its kind has had such ups and downs of fortune. Franklin lived for many years in England, where he was agent... Biographies/History Pages 332

Name	
Email	
Telephone	
Address	
City, State ZIP	

☐ **Credit Card**　　　　☐ **Check / Money Order**

Credit Card Number	
Expiration Date	
Signature	

Please Mail to:　Book Jungle
　　　　　　　　PO Box 2226
　　　　　　　　Champaign, IL 61825
or Fax to:　　　630-214-0564

ORDERING INFORMATION

web: *www.bookjungle.com*
email: *sales@bookjungle.com*
fax: *630-214-0564*
mail: *Book Jungle PO Box 2226 Champaign, IL 61825*
or PayPal *to sales@bookjungle.com*

Please contact us for bulk discounts

DIRECT-ORDER TERMS

**20% Discount if You Order
Two or More Books**
Free Domestic Shipping!
Accepted: Master Card, Visa,
Discover, American Express

www.ingramcontent.com/pod-product-compliance
Lightning Source LLC
Chambersburg PA
CBHW080823020726
47501CB00009B/2403